He Who Goes First

By Kevin J. Curtis

PublishAmerica
Baltimore

© 2004 by Kevin J. Curtis.
All rights reserved. No part of this book may be reproduced, stored in a retrieval system or transmitted in any form or by any means without the prior written permission of the publishers, except by a reviewer who may quote brief passages in a review to be printed in a newspaper, magazine or journal.

First printing

ISBN: 1-4137-4190-8
PUBLISHED BY PUBLISHAMERICA, LLLP
www.publishamerica.com
Baltimore

Printed in the United States of America

Dedicated to the warrior inside…

Acknowledgements:

Thanks to my friend Dave Robinson, for all of your help and for seeing into my vision.

Thanks to my parents, Jim and Char Curtis, for your steadfast support as I continue to struggle with "what I want to be when I grow up."

And finally, thanks to the Minnesota River Valley, for healing my spirit during hard times.

Table of Contents

Chapter 1: The Boy Who Guards Horses 9
Chapter 2: The Emergence 15
Chapter 3: One of Ten 19
Chapter 4: The Blood of Many 25
Chapter 5: Back Among the Living 32
Chapter 6: The Call to Battle 39
Chapter 7: Horse Sense 47
Chapter 8: The Right Fit 52
Chapter 9: Know Thy Enemy 59
Chapter 10: The Edge 67
Chapter 11: All the Way Home 74
Chapter 12: Back in the Saddle 79
Chapter 13: The Enemy Within 87
Chapter 14: The Healing 94
Chapter 15: The Dream World 100
Chapter 16: A New Man 106
Chapter 17: The North 110
Chapter 18: Searching for Answers 117
Chapter 19: Crossing Over 123
Chapter 20: Honored Guests 131
Chapter 21: Homebodies 136
Chapter 22: The Life of a Warrior 142
Chapter 23: The Last Ride 150
Chapter 24: The Aftermath 159

Chapter 1:
The Boy Who Guards Horses

He stood motionless. His eyes were squinting into the sky. Above him, the eagle soared over the steppe. Its flight was effortless as it scanned the barren ground for signs of life. He watched as the bird formed circles in the sky. The shadow from its great wings tore holes in the sunlit ground. Then it happened. Without warning, the giant raptor folded its wings next to its body and shot downward. It hit the earth with a force that seemed to have been sufficient to explode its body into a million parts. Yet when it pumped its wings and climbed back into the sky, it was a small rodent that lay torn and bleeding in the bird's sharp talons. Up, up it flew until it was no longer in view.

The boy went back to his work. He was the guardian of many horses—he and a few other boys. They combed the animals and tended to wounds and damaged hooves. It was an important job, for the men of his tribe depended on horses for all of their needs. The animals transported their nomadic families and were also sometimes a source of food. A warrior may even open a vein in his horse's neck and drink of its lifeblood. The horses also carried the warriors into battle.

This boy had not yet reached the age when he could join the men in conquest…or defeat upon the open plain. He was fast approaching his twelfth summer, and as he rode in mock battle with the other boys, he dreamed of the day that he would join the warriors and return a man with many trophies dangling from his mount. This is the way it is with boys. They regret their youth and fail to see the joy of their innocence and discovery. Too soon they grow up to know the responsibility of being a man. But now, he wished that day would come soon.

The men of his band were drunk on kumiss, and they had retired to their gers with their women. They had returned victorious after raiding a neighboring hostile tribe. These raids had gone on for millennia. Each tribe would take women, animals and goods from the other. It had always been this way since the earliest memories. But word was spreading that a powerful new warlord was binding the tribes together on a new quest. He was taking his armies far from their homeland and conquering distant places and people.

The boy marveled at such a thing. Could it be so? His father had told him about this emerging new order. The men of his clan were in agreement to swear allegiance to this new Khan. To do otherwise would be to risk the anger of this man, and his army was unmatched. It appeared that life was going to change. Many people thought that it would be for the better. Were the old ways so good? Never did a man know when he might be under attack. Never did he know if his sons would be killed or if his wives and daughters would be stolen. Many men had died in these raids. Perhaps it was for the best if the nomads of Mongolia were brought together under one great man. No doubt when united, they would be a force to be reckoned with—beyond the steppe and into the outer world.

The boy was no stranger to death. Life was hard, and he had seen raids and warriors brought back to camp broken and torn open—not unlike the rodent that he had seen in the eagle's grip. His own brother had been killed by the arrow of a gang of boys from a different tribe. He had been hunting with some friends when the boys of an enemy clan ambushed them. Though the fight had been brief, it was violent and deadly. Both sides had lost combatants on that day. The memory clung to the boy as strongly as if it had happened only yesterday. He would avenge his brother's death. It was his duty to his family. But for now, he must tend to the horses. This was also his duty, and vengeance must not be rushed. One who ran into battle unprepared was likely to lose his spirit to the wind. His blood would stain the earth, and he would have to wait to be born again. Patience was a warrior's guide. There would be much time for battle later.

His father had seen many battles and had slain many worthy opponents. He would not have reached the age of 32 summers but for his skill as a warrior. He had many scars, and now his age was showing as he walked with a limp. His woman was 35 summers old, and her wisdom helped to keep her man safe. It was she who counseled him to organize raiding parties when his instinct was to ride into battle alone. He had done so after the death of his son. He had been met by a group of armed warriors from the enemy tribe, and for not the speed of his stallion, the earth would have surely drank his blood on that day.

His father had shown him many things. The boy had become an expert horseman. He was also skilled in the use of weapons for hunting and war. He stood on the brink of manhood, and only time stood in his way from proving himself worthy as a man and a warrior.

He looked back up at the sky. The eagle had returned. It probably had young ones. It would need to find more meat. Then the boy was surprised by the sight of a hawk flying with the eagle. He had never seen such a thing before. Why did the eagle not chase the smaller bird away? Then he remembered the story of how his people had come into existence.

Long ago, it was told that the people of the steppe had come from the taiga farther to the north. They were the descendants of a blue-gray wolf who had taken a fallow deer for his mate. Their first son was named Batachikan, and all of the nomadic people were born of this union. Could it be that the eagle and the hawk might have fallen in love?

He blinked in the bright light as he watched the birds soar through the sky. He wondered why the wolf and deer had a human child. *Perhaps that is what happens in such a union,* he decided. After all, his people were much like the animals. The wolf was wise and powerful. He was not governed by hatred or mercy. Life was as it had always been, and the wolf was masterful in his ability to adapt. His wife, the deer, was beautiful, and this was also true of the women the boy had seen. The story must be true, and the birds that flew above only helped to prove it. He watched them until they again flew beyond his vision. Then, he found himself back on the earth…with the horses. He was still only a boy.

* * * *

Another year had gone by, and the "Boy Who Guards Horses" had grown lean and strong. His father had been gone for a long time. As the warriors returned to their families, he watched the riders and horses approach. There would be much work to do with the horses. He watched for his father, as did his mother a short distance away near the door of the family's ger (felt tent). Many men and horses passed, but not his father. Then the boy recognized his father's horses being led by one of the other men.

The warrior stopped when he reached the boy. He handed the reigns of his father's favorite stallion to him. He also gave the boy the necklace that his father always wore. No words were necessary. The boy saw his mother enter the ger. He took the reigns and the necklace from the warrior, who continued on to his own ger. This boy's father was not going to return. He stood motionless, looking at the dirt and dried blood that was still on the hair of the animal before him. He began to comb the clumps from the horse and clean its coat. He did not weep, though a single tear ran down from the corner of his eye. It left a line down his face where the dust of the steppe had been.

A short time later, the boy sat staring at the necklace that his father had worn for as long as he could remember. The single tooth was very old and had been transformed by age into what appeared to be petrified rock. Though it was worn, it was easily identifiable as a large tooth that had come from a predator. The boy's father had found it when he was a boy. He and his friends had discovered a skeleton buried in the Mongolian desert. The animal had been a relic from the ancient past. The tooth had been meticulously drilled, so as not to break it. It was strung on a piece of sinew. The boy placed the necklace around his own neck.

He was now a man, and he would take his father's place in the next expedition. He would be the lowest in seniority…at least until he proved his valor. If his fate were to die in battle, he would go willingly. Amongst the men of the steppe, this was not questioned. Life had improved under the rule of the Khan. Temuchin was a wise ruler. Those who obeyed him were allowed to live their lives much as they chose. Those who opposed him were mercilessly killed.

The might of the Khan's army was well known. Many cities opened the gates before them. These were spared and were subject to the rule and taxation of the leader, Jenghiz Khan. Any city that decided to fight was left burning, broken, and every person was slaughtered. As word spread, only the mightiest of armies would stand against the Mongols. For the most part, these armies were destroyed and the soldiers were sent fleeing for their lives. The Mongol Hordes were frequently outnumbered by their adversaries, yet any survivor would swear that the Khan's army numbered many more than there actually were. This was the result of the organization born of the great wisdom of Jenghiz Khan, who had a knowledge that came not from books, but rather from an uncanny sense of understanding. The Khan was a master of human nature. His success was also born of the great strength and discipline of his followers.

Jenghiz Khan's armies were organized by tens. One man was in charge of ten, and another man governed ten groups of ten. The result was a force with unmatched communications. The fighting between the tribes had all but stopped. Those who refused to join the Khan were conquered into submission. Never before had a ruler organized the nomadic peoples of the steppe in such a way. The infighting was quelled, and the people now had one purpose—to expand the Khan's influence and territory.

Beyond the notoriety of brute force, the Khan was a fair ruler who treated his soldiers as brothers. He was interested in the goods, technology and ways of all those cultures he met and/or conquered. The trading of goods was paramount to his expansion, and he never forgot his own lack of formal education. He enjoyed the company of scholars, and he insisted that his own children be educated.

Formal education was not the destiny of the boy who had now become a man. It was his fate to be a soldier. He and others like him, on sturdy horses, would overwhelm much of the civilized world in a way that had never been done before…and would never be again.

Chapter 2:
The Emergence

Much time had passed, and the boy was now a man known as, "Wind Rider." He had a good eye for horses, and he could pick the fastest steeds from any herd. He was an expert horseman, and he spent much of his time training for battle. By this time, he had participated in many fierce battles as a soldier in the army of Jenghiz Khan. On one particular day, far from the steppe of his youth, he and his brothers made ready for an attack.

The messenger rode back to the waiting army. He fell from his mount at the feet of his commander. An arrow was lodged in his back, and he whispered the words that the inhabitants of the city would not yield to the Khan. He coughed blood and gave his spirit to the wind. The general gave a cry of vengeance, which rang out repeatedly as it was carried by tens, hundreds and thousands until the mass of men on horseback thundered ahead. Artillery was brought forward on two-wheel carts, and the barrage began. For hours, the walls of the city were bombarded by catapults, until they caved-in to the onslaught.

Wind Rider was among the first to rush through the opening. His sword was wet with blood as he and his comrades killed every living thing within the walls of the city. He and his horse were doused by blood, as they dashed about and hacked apart the living and the dead. The fight was over quickly. The soldiers who tried to protect the city were no match for the army of the great Khan. Some fought bravely to their deaths while others begged for their lives as they were cut down.

The victorious plundered the city, and anything that was left behind was soon turned into a burning inferno. There was no remorse for the fallen. Had they been wise, they would not have stood against the Khan. The Mongols were as their ruler was. They were uncorrupted by hatred or mercy. Like the wolf who had first fathered the nomads, they lived by the laws of the strong dominating the weak. Like the wolf, they banded together to ensure their survival.

As day gave way to night, the men celebrated with kumiss and told stories. They sharpened weapons and cared for injuries and their horses. The scouts had reported that a nearby king was calling together a vast army. They were already in route to meet the Khan's soldiers in battle. With sentries to watch the night, the warriors slept. Sleep was a weapon to a soldier. One who had not slept was likely to make a mistake that could cost him his life. The fall of one could lead to the fall of many. For this reason, the men tried to rest.

In the morning, they ate from the spoils of the previous day's conquest. Then the order came to mount up. They would ride forward to meet the opposing army. The scouts had identified a battlefield, and it was in this place that the commanders would bring their men. Much blood would be spilled this day in the name of the Khan of Water, for Jenghiz had taken the name which identified him as the ruler associated with the strength, endurance and flexibility of water. Like an ocean, his army was poised to swallow the enemy whole.

The sun was high in the sky, and the Mongols maneuvered to put their backs to it. The battlefield was large, and it would be a good place to spill the blood of their opponents. Wind Rider saw the eagle riding the wind currents above. The bird would be a witness to the great power of the Khan's army. The men were eager to do battle, though they waited patiently for the order. This was an army that used speed and organization to undo their enemies.

Wind Rider tested his bow. The pull of the Mongol bow was beyond the abilities of most other men. The Khan's soldiers were a mass of trained muscle, and they could bend the bows with relative ease. They used two bows—one for distance and one for short range. The power of these weapons was so great that it was possible for a

Mongol arrow to pass through one man and kill the man next to him. Despite this fact, most of the Khan's soldiers preferred the sword. Their agility and swift horses propelled them into their enemies' lines and spread panic and death to all those who opposed them.

Just before midday, the army of the enemy king arrived at the site of their undoing. Their commanders lined the men up according to their tasks. The archers would shower the enemy with arrows and then the call to charge would be made. It was all very predictable. It was the way wars were fought.

The Mongols were not bound to the rules of decorum, and they were all expert archers and swordsmen. When the battle began, they too rained arrows down on the opposing army. Soon the cry went through their ranks to retreat! The enemy generals were surprised by how easily they had routed the Khan's army, and they gave the order to pursue. The enemy stretched their ranks deep into the territory that had formerly been controlled by the nomads. With lightening speed, the Mongols reversed their tactics and turned toward their opponents and charged them. The king's army found itself flanked, and the Khan's horse-soldiers rushed in to attack. Screams were heard up into the sky where the eagle still soared above the carnage.

Wind Rider had been the first to wield his horse into the enemy. He had already cut down several surprised enemy soldiers before his ranks closed around him and the ground was showered with blood and body parts. The king's generals were in shock as they saw their troops dispatched so quickly. They called a retreat and spurred their horses to escape certain death.

Wind Rider saw them. His horse was swift, and he kicked its ribs and sailed over the mass of fallen bodies. He had one purpose now, and he focused on his prey like a wolf giving chase. He reached the closest group of officers and swung his sword. The general, still on his mount, was nearly decapitated as Wind Rider's sword continued to cut through the terrified men. At full gallop, he armed his bow and fired arrows into the leaders who had been on the far side of the battlefield. His comrades had captured the last of the officers and unceremoniously cut them down.

The battle was now little more than a slaughter. The enemies had no leaders, no organization, and they were completely terrified. The Khan's generals watched as their men completed the task at hand. Before long, they called a halt to the operation, and they spared one young man from the king's fallen army. This man was given a horse and a message. "Tell your king what happened here today," the general said. The victorious Mongols watched as the terrified man rode his horse hard and soon disappeared from sight.

This battle was over, and the losses were very lopsided. The Khan's army had only taken a few casualties, while the enemy army lay on the battlefield crushed and bleeding. This was very typical of their handiwork. The Khan's army was feared wherever they went. On this day, the commanders noted the bravery and skill of one who goes first. Wind Rider was about to receive a new name and rank.

Chapter 3:
One of Ten

It was what would later be called a "battlefield commission." Wind Rider was called before the top commanders of the army. He was asked to sit and was offered food and drink. He was also asked to join in the discussion about the victory that had been bestowed upon them. Though the evening had become cold, he was warmed from the inside by the honor that was his, in the company of the greatest of the Khan's warriors. He had been welcomed into the inner circle as a brother.

They spoke seriously about the battle and the tactics that had been so successful. It was intoxicating to hear the other men speak of his deeds on the battlefield—of how he was first into the fray and how he cut down the commanders of the enemy army. Their undoing had propelled him into the good graces of his own commanders, who were now his hosts. It was almost as if he were in the company of the Khan himself!

Kumiss was brought, and the fermented mare's milk began to loosen the serious edge of the conversation. Laughter filled the night from not only this spot, but from around the entire encampment. The stars shown brightly in celebration of their victory. The spirits had smiled on these men and their Khan. Life was good at this moment. The camaraderie of these men was proof of the Khan's greatness and wisdom. Men, who in previous generations would have been enemies, sat together under the stars on this night. Their unification had created an army that was, as of yet, unmatched on any battlefield.

Yet, beyond the firelight of the circle of leaders, something burned in the night. It was the hatred in the heart of a single man. He was jealous of the man who had been called Wind Rider. Why had he been elevated? Had not many men participated in this victory? Had not Soonok also killed men today? Was the son of the man who killed his father worthy of this honor?

Even as Wind Rider received his new name of, "He-Who-Goes-First," Soonok wished him dead. Word had spread that the man with the new name would be a leader of ten in the next battle. Yet this was not the greatest insult Soonok would have to endure. That was yet to come. His heart burned with envy and hate.

Meanwhile, He-Who-Goes-First was accepted into the leadership with great joy and laughter. These were men who knew of death and appreciated the joys of life when responsibility permitted it. Tonight was such a time. It had been a glorious battle for all. The Khan would be very pleased with their victory. Amidst the frivolity, He-Who-Goes-First was told that he would accompany a group of messengers who would be traveling to see Jenghiz Khan. They would be carrying assorted treasures and goods, and the new leader of ten would even get the chance to meet the Khan. Soon, he would visit the great palace of the Mongol ruler, and tonight's celebration would be as a grain of sand is to a mountain.

The next day, at first light, the group would depart. This was an honor he could scarcely comprehend. Even as a boy he had never dared to imagine such a thing could happen to him. His father would be very proud. As he dreamed that night, his father's spirit came to him and spoke words that were like a two-edged sword.

"He-Who-Goes-First," his father's spirit said, "will be honored by many…and hated by few. Watch your back, my son."

The spirit disappeared into the night, and all that could be heard in the camp were the snores of sleeping men.

The following morning, He-Who-Goes-First and a small group of messengers and pack horses departed for the Khan's palace. It took many days to travel the distance. Along the way they were occasionally met by potentially hostile men. They carried the seal of Jenghiz Khan, however, and most of the men who saw it were afraid to tamper with messengers of the Khan.

When they finally reached their destination, He-Who-Goes-First was overwhelmed by the size and opulence of the palace. He was a nomad, a herder, a hunter and a warrior. He was not accustomed to gold, jewels, and the fabulous cloths that he now saw. The messengers were taken before the Khan, while He-Who-Goes-First was shown to a room. He was offered food, drink and women, and he indulged himself as he never had before. It was the next morning when he was summoned to the Khan.

He quickly washed himself and put on the new garments that had been lain out for him. He was led down a magnificent hall, and then he entered a large room where he was offered a seat near the Khan. He maintained his composure, though he felt a bit lightheaded. He wasn't sure if it was the excesses of the previous night or if it was his nervousness. To his great relief, the Khan was pleasant and interested in the new leader of ten.

Food and drink were brought, and for their entertainment, a number of wrestling matches took place. The Khan also had musicians and magicians who performed for the group that had assembled. It was a delightful time, and He-Who-Goes-First was not sure what wonders he would see next.

As the hours passed, the Khan asked him if he had any requests before he returned to his new position within the army. He-Who-Goes-First had not seen his wife for a long time. He asked if he could go to her. The Khan smiled and nodded his head. Of course, this was something that he should do. He-Who-Goes-First thanked the Khan for all of his kindness. Then he was led back to his room. The next morning, he was again given new clothes. As he prepared to leave, he was given new weapons and armor. When he was led outside of the palace, he was presented with seven new horses in addition to the three that he had brought with him. He was also given two escorts to accompany him on his journey home.

On military campaigns, the Mongols sometimes brought their families at the rear of their army. Being nomadic people, this was not any great hardship. The Khan's forces had now traveled such distances, however, that this was no longer a practical way of doing things. Because of this, He-Who-Goes-First's wife Gerka was far from the army that was to be his ultimate destination. She lived in a village that was completely mobile and followed the seasonal grazing patterns of their livestock.

When he arrived at the village, He-Who-Goes-First met his wife at the door of her ger. She had had a daughter in his absence, and he was delighted when he saw the baby. He spent several wonderful days and nights with his family before he set off to rejoin his comrades in the faraway lands. He took several of his horses and departed from the village. His wife looked on from the door of her ger, holding the baby as her husband rode away.

Accompanying him was a boy of about twelve summers. The boy had been orphaned, and He-Who-Goes-First took him as his son and assistant. As a man who now possessed rank and many horses, he could use the boy's help. The boy looked to this man for guidance, and together they rode toward the far reaches of the Khan's empire. They traveled for many days until they reached the army's camp.

He was greeted with much joy and presented with his ten. The men were all eager to please their new captain—all except for one. His insult was realized when he was chosen to serve under He-Who-Goes-First, for this man was one who had much hate in his heart for the young leader. Grudgingly, he showed insincere respect when he joined the ranks. They were prepared to train for their next campaign. He-Who-Goes-First led them in battle drills. He was pleased with his men and with their prowess. He noticed one, however, who seemed to be occupied with some other agenda. He would need to work to bring this man in line for the good of the ten.

During the drilling, the man named Soonok came very close to wounding his commander in a sword exercise. It became clear to He-Who-Goes-First that this man had some sort of dislike of him. This behavior served no one, and he approached the man and asked him to air his grievance. Soonok replied that he, not He-Who-Goes-First, should be leading the drills. This was obviously a challenge, and He-Who-Goes-First immediately organized his men for training in wrestling. He matched them by size and paired himself against Soonok. To lose this match could seriously undermine his authority, but He-Who-Goes-First was an excellent wrestler.

When their turn came, Soonok and He-Who-Goes-First locked up in a battle for leverage. Both men were of great strength, and the technical match began to grow more violent. Soonok had lashed out with his fists and bloodied the nose of his commander. He smiled at the blood, thinking that he would win this match. He-Who-Goes-First countered him with a vertical flip that left his opponent gasping as the breath was knocked from his lungs. Both men lay on the ground panting, and He-Who-Goes-First regained his footing first.

Soonok would not yield, and again the two men locked up, muscle against muscle in combat. As the two combatants continued, the sky began to open up, and rain now poured down. Inside the circle of men, the two wrestlers continued, even as the thunder and lightening began.

The entirety of the army was somewhat alarmed by the storm, for it had come quickly, and they knew of the dangers of the fire from the sky. Yet, the circle began to grow larger as other groups of ten became mesmerized by the level of competition that was unfolding before them. They draped skins over themselves to shed the rain…and then the hail which began to pelt the ground and the men.

The two fighters seemed oblivious to both the fury of the storm and the audience that had gathered. Soon they were also oblivious to the rules of wrestling, which had been designed to spare injuries. The generals also looked on. They knew their new protégé would have to prove himself worthy to lead in the eyes of his men. This was only one of many challenges that the young warrior would face if he continued his journey to the top of the ranks.

Bleeding, covered in mud and drenched from the deluge, it seemed that neither combatant could win this bout. Yet they continued on, bruised and exhausted. Then it hit. The lightening bolt crashed from the heavens down to the earth of the mortals who were now caught in the full fury of the storm. The tingling sensation was felt by all, as the electricity leapt into the ground. The force of the blast had left some of the men dazed, and when the smoke and steam cleared, He-Who-Goes-First was picking himself off of the ground. Nearby, Soonok was lying near death, with burns visible across his body.

The crowd was amazed by the spectacle. He-Who-Goes-First went to his fallen foe and lifted the man into his arms. He carried him to the shelter of his tent and ordered his men to see to his wounds. As quickly as it had happened, the storm subsided, and before long, the sun shone on the evening horizon.

He-Who-Goes-First would not talk that night. He was in deep meditation, and he was sitting in vigil near the tent that held Soonok. The healer had been inside for a long while, and he came out and said that the man would recover. He-Who-Goes-First was grateful for the report, and his demeanor improved.

The talk among the men of the army was hushed, yet all knew what had happened. After confronting his commander, Soonok had been struck down by the god of the sky. He-Who-Goes-First must have great power to cause such a thing to happen. Still, Soonok lived. How could this be? Men had been known to have been hit by the fire from the sky, and horses or other livestock too. Yet, most often, the man or beast did not survive. Whether or not death came swiftly or crept up during the night, few had lived after such a blow.

Would Soonok also be killed as death rethought his injuries? Did Soonok possess some power that could prevent the fire from the sky from burning him to death? There was much fear, awe and conjecture that night. All were affected in some way by the events that had transpired on that day.

He-Who-Goes-First finished the food that the boy who took care of his horses had brought for him. As he drifted to sleep, the boy cleaned the wounds of his new stepfather. He-Who-Goes-First did not wake up even from the pain of his wounds. Though he had not succumbed to his opponent, exhaustion had taken him. The night was silent, though off in the distance, an occasional rumble of thunder could be heard. The storm was playing more tricks on the night in some other land far off in the darkness.

Chapter 4:
The Blood of Many

Life returned to normal as Soonok was carried back to his village on horseback. He had recovered well from his near-death experience, though he would not be useful to the army for some time. While on expedition, a man in his condition was only a liability, and so he was sent home. Another more agreeable man was brought into the ten to replace him. With this incident behind him, He-Who-Goes-First found his new position much more satisfying.

His ten were ready for battle, and he felt that he could trust each one as a brother. Their test was soon to come. They were about to meet another army even greater than the last. The Khan's generals were fearless and confident in their soldiers' abilities. The intelligence reports from reconnaissance indicated that the army that had been brought together to repel the Mongol force was comprised of the armies of three kings. The Khan's troops were outnumbered by five to one.

Undaunted, they pushed forward and eagerly anticipated the fight. There was no time to secure the battlefield and seek the aid of the sun or the elevations. When they found the enemy army, the soldiers were already charging downhill, sun to their backs. A lesser force would have been overwhelmed, but the commanders of the Khan's warriors issued their orders, and the Mongol army separated and rushed parallel to the scrimmage line as they shot arrows into the enemy forces at full gallop.

Half of the Mongol force went left, and the other half to the right, with a precision that was previously unknown to war. In minutes, they had nearly surrounded the less organized army of the three kings. Arrows flew from all directions, and the frightened soldiers inflicted much damage to their own forces, as the Mongols continued to cut their enemies into small groups that were dispatched quickly and efficiently.

The larger army was fragmented, and communication with their leaders was cut off. Many tried to flee, but most ran into the waiting Mongol wall that had flanked them and blocked their retreat. In typical fashion, He-Who-Goes-First and his ten had been among the first to enter the fray. They watched each other's backs as they cut their way through the opposition and spilled the blood of many into the thirsty ground. The smell of blood and death was strong in the air now as the final killing was finished. The few who survived the battle returned to their kings, swearing that the Mongols' number was ten times what it actually was.

The swiftness and organization of the Khan's army often made their numbers seem far greater than they were. Still, this misinformation only proved to benefit the Mongols as it worked to instill terror in others who may have stood against them. Many kings and rulers were swayed not to do battle for fear of the Mongols' reputation alone. Many cities opened their gates to the Khan's forces and willingly became his subjects. In return, they gained protection by becoming part of the Khan's empire. By obeying and paying tribute, they were allowed to live in peace.

Jenghiz Khan was interested in trade, and he enjoyed learning about the goods and the ways of those he conquered. Great caravans were traveling the "Silk Road," with the blessing of the Khan. His influence was far reaching, and his military power had reduced the lawlessness that had preceded his rule. Certainly one of his greatest legacies was in the trading of goods and knowledge over vast distances.

As the battle came to an end, the Khan's warriors made camp. He-Who-Goes-First had not lost any of his ten. It had been a good day for the men and their leader. It was a good day for the nomads of the steppe and for their Khan. They had surrounded the enemy like their ancestor the wolf. They had separated their frightened quarry and defeated them on the battlefield. This was their duty and their birthright.

* * * *

To the Khan's army, war was a way of life. The knowledge that one's soul was immortal was comforting to those who saw their comrades fall in battle. Spiritual bonds were stronger than the bonds of flesh in their society. It was normal for the warriors to consider each other brothers, and the Khan was like a great father to the men. Great acts of bravery and selflessness were born of this allegiance to the Khan and to one another.

There was also a sense of pride in the empire that they were helping to create. The soldiers were eager to do battle. Many lands and cities were taken without a fight, as the Khan's army marched further into new territories. But battles were common, and always there was a ruler somewhere who was willing to send his forces against the Khan's army.

On one such day, He-Who-Goes-First led his ten into a fearsome battle near the shore of a great lake. The water began to turn red as the battle waged. While he was occupied in a violent confrontation by sword, He-Who-Goes-First jumped from his horse and took the fight to the enemy on foot.

There was much confusion, and the dust and blood flowed freely on that day. Just as the battle reached its full fury, He-Who-Goes-First was bludgeoned across the back of his head. The force of the blow sent him face first to the ground. Blood gushed from his head, and his skull had been fractured. It was only seconds before he lost consciousness. His ten had seen the assault, and the man responsible literally lost his head as one of the Mongol swords ripped through his throat and out the other side. The ten fought bravely, and they rescued their leader before returning to finish the slaughter.

* * * *

He-Who-Goes-First was spinning through a brilliantly illuminated tunnel. He could not feel his limbs as he was carried along through space and time. The blood was gone, as was the battle and the armies. He was quite sure that he must be dead. He thought about Gerka and their daughter. How he wished that he could hold them both again. He should not be surprised by his own death, though he certainly hadn't expected it to come on this day. He felt only a dull pain in his head as he was pulled upward.

His sense of time and space was altered, and he did not know where he was or where he was going. Before long, he found himself lying next to the water. He turned to drink, but his thirst was not quenched. Had he been sent to the wrong place? He pondered his predicament for a moment before he was greeted by the vision of his father. He asked the apparition where he was, and his father motioned for He-Who-Goes-First to follow. He slowly got up and watched as his father disappeared into the water.

He-Who-Goes-First began to walk into the body of water that his father had gone into. He was surprised to find that the water was warm, and as it rose over his head, he did not hold his breath but rather breathed the liquid into his lungs where the warmth continued to spread inside of him. His father was gone, but he found himself wandering through a city that was completely submerged. It was inhabited by a race that seemed to be half-human and half-fish.

Ahead he saw a palace that reminded him of the palace of Jenghiz Khan…the Khan of the water. Perhaps he would find the Khan there! He was unsure of anything, except that he wanted to go to that palace. As he continued, a porpoise came close, and he reached out and put his hand on its dorsal fin. The porpoise increased speed as it pulled He-Who-Goes-First along. The speed was intoxicating, and He-Who-Goes-First pulled himself onto the animal as if he were riding a horse.

Great schools of fish went by as the porpoise continued on toward the palace. Many wonders were in this city, and He-Who-Goes-First noticed a shell of a size he had never seen before. It was perhaps larger than ten men, and it was the color of the sky. The palace up ahead glowed with a white light, and the porpoise continued on. He-Who-Goes-First attempted to speak to the animal, but the water drowned his words, and no sound could be heard.

When they reached the golden walkway near the palace door, the porpoise stopped, and He-Who-Goes-First stepped down from its back. The animal glanced back and then shot forward and vanished through a curtain of aquatic plants. He-Who-Goes-First walked to the door of the palace, and it opened before him. He stepped inside, but the darkness prevented him from seeing. Slowly, his vision adapted to the dark interior, and he found a staircase that he knew he must climb. He began his ascent, but he was still unable to see to the top. After much time had passed, he finally came to the water's surface.

As he left the warmth of the liquid, he felt the coolness of the air. He emerged from the water completely dry! He found himself at the base of a tall mountain, and he began to climb. His progress was effortless, as the effects of gravity seemed to be less than what he was used to. He was aware of a dull throbbing in his head as he continued to climb. Up he went over rocks, scrub trees and boulders. He scaled a sheer rock wall using only his arms. He was not sure what was ahead, but he felt that he must reach the top.

When he finally came to the peak, he saw a mass of branches that were woven together. He grabbed onto the edge and pulled himself over the side. He landed in a depression and found himself face-to-face with a golden eagle that was twice as big as a horse! The bird looked at him like he was so much meat, and then it spoke.

"Why have you come here?"

"I am He-Who-Goes-First. I was killed in a great battle for the Khan."

"You are not dead," said the eagle.

"Then where am I?"

"You have entered the 'other world,'" the eagle answered.

"Yet I am alive?"

"You cannot stay here; you must climb onto my back."

He-Who-Goes-First climbed onto the back of the eagle, and the great bird left the nest and pumped its great wings as it sailed up and up into the sky. He-Who-Goes-First held tightly to the great feathers of the bird's neck as they flew ever higher.

From the back of the eagle, He-Who-Goes-First soon gained confidence enough to look down from this great height. The speed and ease with which they soared was exhilarating, and he could see farther than he ever had before. Below he saw herders and fishermen and those who tended the soil. He saw battles and castles and lands with strange people and stranger animals.

"What is this?" he asked. "Is this the land I used to know?"

"Hmmm…" said the eagle. "It is, and it is not."

"I do not understand," said He-Who-Goes-First.

"On your left side," the eagle began, "is what has been. To the right is what will be. We are traveling across time at an angle."

"How can this be?" asked He-Who-Goes-First.

"One who lives in an iron chair to the right says it is 'imaginary time.' There is more to the universe than you can understand as a man, and there is more to the universe than the universe itself."

"Are we in the middle…are we in what is 'now'?" asked He-Who-Goes-First.

"Yes. Space and time are connected as water is connected to land. We are traveling between what was and what is yet to be. To you, neither one exists, because you live between the two. Here in the other world, all exist together," replied the eagle.

Above, He-Who-Goes-First saw a great ocean of blood. Inside its turbulent waters he could see parts of men flailing and screaming. The sight was horrific—even to one who had participated in much carnage on the battlefield. He was afraid to ask the eagle about it, but the bird responded anyway.

"It is 'The Blood of Many.'"

The eagle kept flying, and from this great height, He-Who-Goes-First could see that the world appeared to be a great rock or sphere. The eagle began to turn, and below, He-Who-Goes-First saw his village. Below him was the ger of his wife. The eagle shook him from its back, and He-Who-Goes-First could feel himself falling.

Down he fell for what seemed like a very long time. He did not know if he would be crushed when he hit the earth or if the "magic" that had carried him this far would continue.

Below, he saw the ger. It was hers…his beloved wife's. He was falling directly on top of her tent, and he was suddenly overcome by the fear that he might crush her. When he finally hit the top, he passed right through the material and was lying on the bed inside. He opened his eyes. His wife Gerka sat looking at him. She did not speak, but tears were running down her face. Her husband had returned from the other world, and he was alive!

Chapter 5:
Back Among the Living

It was several more days before He-Who-Goes-First was able to walk. At first, even to sit up made him nauseous and caused his head to throb. The bleeding had stopped, and the bump had gone down significantly. The dark rings under his eyes were beginning to fade, and he was starting to put back the weight he had lost while he was comatose. Basically, he was still a mess, but he was getting better.

He was restless. He did not like feeling helpless. He was, however, glad to have the time with Gerka and their daughter. For too long he had missed them, and the little girl was growing bigger each day. He played with her inside of the ger, and her laughter and hugs were great medicine for him. He had, it seemed, cheated death. His head was healing, and he was soon playing with his daughter outside of the ger.

At first, his eyes were sensitive to the sunlight, but as the hours and days passed, he grew stronger. Soon he was walking around the encampment, and before long, he was repairing his weapons and discussing the future with the boy who he had adopted as his son. The boy had brought his father back to the village after his near-death injury. The army was in the middle of a campaign, and it was safer to send He-Who-Goes-First back with the boy and their horses than it was to try to bring the fallen warrior with the soldiers.

At first it was thought that he would die anyway, but the boy insisted that he should be allowed to take He-Who-Goes-First back to their village. It was a long journey for a boy of his age, but he had proven himself to be a man in his abilities. His loyalty to the man who had taken him in was without question. He had only left his injured father's side when Gerka was with him or to take care of the horses. Now, while his body mended, He-Who-Goes-First began to share with the boy the knowledge that he had learned from his own father.

He-Who-Goes-First coached his son in the making and repairing of weapons. He showed him the proper care of horses, and as he grew stronger, he showed the boy how to shoot his bow accurately and how to use the sword. He-Who-Goes-First had gone through his weaponry and found his old sword, which he gave to his son. He also replaced the boy's bow with a "man's bow." The look on the young man's face was all the thanks needed. It was obviously an important day for them both. The boy began to practice his marksmanship with renewed zeal. He was able to hit his target with nearly every shot, whether it was moving or stationary.

Gerka was pleased to have her man back with her. She loved the smell of his body and how it made her feel safe. She enjoyed having the boy around too, and she was grateful for his help and for how he had adopted the little girl as his sister. He took great joy in making his little sister laugh, and she was always looking for her big brother. The days and nights were the happiest that Gerka could ever remember. She wished that things could stay this way forever. She knew, however, that hers was the life of the wife of a soldier. She knew her husband would return to the army when he was healed.

He-Who-Goes-First was also enjoying his time recuperating, despite his physical limitations. He was prone to over-exercising, and both his wife and his son had to remind him that he needed to take it easy. His family was well aware of the changes that lay ahead once he was well again. This was perhaps another reason that they wanted him to slow down.

As much as he was feeling the draw of battle, He-Who-Goes-First was also enjoying this period of domesticity. He had a family that any man would be proud of. When he looked into the beautiful eyes of his wife, he felt only joy. She was the most beautiful woman he had ever seen, and he lay awake sometimes listening to her breathing as she slept with her head on his shoulder. Perhaps this was the spiritual reason for his injury. He had simply been away for too long.

He-Who-Goes-First reflected on the curious memories left over by the dreams he had while he lay near death. Was it a message? Was it his imagination? It did not matter. To him, it all seemed real. He had learned that as what was yet to come traveled into what already was, the choices he made in the now could affect the future. It was exciting and sobering all at once. The concept was so large that it hurt his injured head to think about it. Could the sword one chose or the horse one rode influence his destiny? Perhaps it could and perhaps not. Maybe it didn't even matter. He was a soldier, and he would return to the army, and one day he would return as the leader of ten.

It was good to have this time to think, he decided. It was good to have this time with his family. It was good to be back among the living.

* * * *

After many weeks of recuperating, He-Who-Goes-First was finally ready to rejoin the army. He and the boy prepared the horses and their supplies and readied for their journey. Gerka watched sadly as they prepared to go. As always, she stood in the door of her ger as they rode away. She dreaded these moments, and though she tried not to think about it, she couldn't help but wonder if her husband would ever return to her.

Back on his horse again, He-Who-Goes-First felt both remorse about leaving his wife and daughter and the anticipation of rejoining the army. He was still getting stronger every day, but he could not wait forever. His was the life of a warrior, and he would rejoin his brothers in conquest in the name of the Khan.

They had traveled far when a small group of heavily armed men approached them. Their leader wore a metal helmet, and he was a full head and shoulders taller than the others were. The boy had a bad feeling about these men, and so did his father. He-Who-Goes-

First did not understand their language, but it soon became apparent that these men meant to steal their horses. With six of them and only He-Who-Goes-First and the boy, the odds of keeping their horses or their lives weren't very good. Still, they would not yield to the strangers. Fortunately, the pride of the other men was greater than their wisdom.

The leader provoked a fight with He-Who-Goes-First. Each man dismounted and faced the other. The other men surrounded the two, and the boy stayed close but remained with the horses. He took full advantage of the commotion and secretly readied his bow. He would need all of his skill and speed if there was any hope that he and his father would survive the rest of this day.

The helmeted giant moved toward He-Who-Goes-First. His giant arm held an equally giant sword, which he swung vigorously at his opponent. His huge shield was held close, to repel the blows of He-Who-Goes-First. The clang of metal rang out, as did the chants and taunts of the men who watched. They had seen this spectacle many times before, and they were all sure that no man could defeat their leader. He swung again, and the sword glanced off the shield of He-Who-Goes-First and cut through the thigh of the Mongol. The boy grimaced, wanting to shoot his arrows yet hoping for the right moment when he and his father could work together to vanquish these enemies.

The giant laughed and taunted some more. He was enjoying this. More than once, He-Who-Goes-First thought that he might see the other world again, but somehow he managed to stay out of reach of the fatal blow. After more time had passed, He-Who-Goes-First noticed that his adversary appeared to be growing tired. His large size must require an immense amount of energy to move at this level of competition. Like a wolf watching his prey, the boy noticed it too. They may yet live through this fight, he thought.

The weight of the great sword showed as the giant continued to hack at the shield and armor of He-Who-Goes-First. In an instant, the huge man had left himself open to attack, and the swift sword of He-Who-Goes-First found its mark. The giant bellowed as his side between his armor was punctured. The other men saw their leader's predicament, and as the first man moved to his aid, an arrow pierced through his neck, and he dropped to the ground, gasping as his blood mixed with the air he was trying to breathe.

The boy reloaded and fired again. His aim was good, and he shot above the armor and sent his arrow into the back of the second man's head, right where the head and neck came together and just below where his helmet covered. Death came instantly. He reloaded as another man lunged at him. This man was pierced through the eye by the projectile, and the boy was now three-for-three!

He-Who-Goes-First swung around and nearly took the head off of the fourth man with one well-placed swing of his sword. There were only two left now, and the giant was feeling the effects of his blood and bowels draining through the wound in his side. He-Who-Goes-First finished him with a stab of his sword through the giant's mouth. The sword broke through the big man's teeth and emerged out the other side.

The last man went for the boy, and successfully blocked the oncoming arrow with his shield. The boy kicked his horse and the animal galloped to safety as the assailant now turned to face an annoyed He-Who-Goes-First. The man began to back away, and the boy charged him on horseback. He leveled his sword at the animal, and his face was cut just above the nose horizontally as He-Who-Goes-First finished him with his sword.

The boy jumped from his mount and began to treat the wound that the giant had inflicted on his father's leg. It was only a minor injury, and they smiled at each other as they took inventory of the weapons, supplies and horses that they had just acquired. The dead would be food for scavengers. They deserved nothing more. They had attempted to kill and steal from a smaller force, and they had been unworthy of victory. The boy took the giant's helmet as a souvenir. It might be valuable to trade. It was not something that He-Who-Goes-First would wear. This helmet was cumbersome and impeded vision. It was also too large for the head of most men.

The two victors continued on their way. He-Who-Goes-First was proud of his son. He had battled well, and his marksmanship was uncanny. Truly this boy was becoming a man of exceptional abilities. The boy radiated under the praise of He-Who-Goes-First. His father was a great warrior. He had killed a giant! They had quite a nice supply of horses now. It had been a good day after all. Best of all, they were still among the living.

* * * *

It was a long trip to find their way to the Khan's army. By the time He-Who-Goes-First and his son found where the army had been, it had moved again. They were traveling farther and farther to the west. It was a very dangerous journey through a mostly hostile territory. Usually a group of two would not be traveling such a distance alone.

Danger came in many forms, and it was not only human beings that could be deadly. The land was harsh, and the desert was always difficult to pass. He-Who-Goes-First made sure that they had enough water for the journey. Despite the best efforts to prepare for unforeseen difficulties, the risks were always there. One thing that was never predictable was the weather.

Late one afternoon as the two travelers made their way across the vast sand dunes, the sky began to grow prematurely dark. He-Who-Goes-First noticed the change in the weather, and he told the boy that they needed to find a place to wait out the approaching storm. There was an eerie stillness at that moment, but the older man knew that this would soon change.

They tethered their horses on long ropes, to give the animals room to move. Then the warrior and his son covered themselves with a blanket, and they held it tightly as the wind began to increase. Before long, the roar became deafening, and despite the blanket, the sand was blowing furiously into the eyes, nose and mouth of the two Mongols. The sand behaved as if it was a living demon, and the two soon found themselves in danger of being buried by the wicked storm.

The wind and blowing sand continued for a long time, and only after nightfall were the man and boy able to dig themselves out.

They were not completely covered, but they had been partially buried as the dunes blew apart and redeveloped. The horses seemed to have survived fairly well, but when the first light of morning came, He-Who-Goes-First decided to use some of their precious water to help to clean the animals' eyes.

The sand and dust had coated everything, including He-Who-Goes-First and his son. The dust stuck to their skin and itched inside of their clothes. The landscape had changed its look and shape overnight, and the rising sun was their only guide to place them in the right direction. This journey had been wrought with challenges, and the boy began to wonder if they would ever find the army at all. He decided to leave the giant's helmet out in the desert, in case it was bringing bad luck. Then, two days after the storm had passed, they saw a vast gathering of men and horses directly in front of them. They had finally made it out of the deadly sand and back among the living.

Chapter 6:
The Call to Battle

They were welcomed back to the army with much joy. It was good to be back with their brothers. There were a few uncomfortable moments when He-Who-Goes-First rejoined his ten. There was a new leader in his absence, and how this would be remedied with the return of the former leader was uncertain. The moment passed quickly, when He-Who-Goes-First took his place with the ten and conceded leadership. He would have time to regain his position later. There were more battles ahead, and he would either prove worthy, or he would not. The new leader was his friend, and the current situation would not change that.

He-Who-Goes-First had returned to the ranks during a period of rest, and the men entertained themselves with contests, wrestling and horse races. The boy was frequently occupied with contests of his archery skills. It seemed that no matter who he competed against, no man was able to match his skill with the bow. He became known as Straight Arrow, and he was pleased with his new name. His archery skills made him a valued addition to the Khan's army. At just thirteen summers of age, he was quickly gaining much notoriety.

The other men looked after the boy because he would be called upon to use his skills strategically during battle. His marksmanship would be used to eliminate battlefield leaders, which would leave the opposing army in a state of chaos. This would be of great benefit to the Khan's army. He-Who-Goes-First was very proud of his son. He had found the boy as an orphan, and Straight Arrow had proven himself worthy as a warrior and as a son.

Father and son had gained many horses with wagers over the boy's skill with the bow. Soon, however, the other men saw that such wagers were futile, and no one would bet against the Khan's newest marksman. As he exercised with the other soldiers, Straight Arrow became lean and strong. He also proved to be wise beyond his years. He was very interested in battle tactics, and he liked to sit just outside of the circle of the generals while they talked. His presence was both noted and accepted, though he had not yet been asked to join the circle. Nor would he have been so bold as to ask for such an honor. He was content with his position and thankful for his good fortune.

He-Who-Goes-First was rapidly regaining his strength, quickness and agility. Since his injury, he had exercised and trained hard. He was once again among the best wrestlers in the ranks, and few men would have dared to challenge him with the sword. His talents as a swordsman were equal with his son's skills with the bow. Together, they were a deadly combination, as those who challenged them on their trip to rejoin the army had found out too late.

As armies on campaign do, the men were starting to get anxious for a fight. The order came to mount up. They were heading into battle. By evening, they were in place across from a massive army that had been sent to stop their advance. As darkness came, they realized that things would not begin until early the next day. There was a tension throughout both camps. It was hard to sit and do nothing when battle loomed so near.

When morning came, He-Who-Goes-First took his place among his group of ten. Straight Arrow stayed close to the generals, waiting for his orders. The enemy troops were in place across the battlefield, and the Mongols were mounted and ready. The order came from the other side first, and with the sound of trumpets, the charge began. The Mongols waited as the enemy force closed the gap. Then the order for their advance came. He-Who-Goes-First stayed near the rear, for he knew the tactic of the day. With the first rain of arrows, the Mongol force began their retreat. They dashed toward the rear on speedy horses. He-Who-Goes-First retreated slowly, leaving him near the front of the skirmish line.

As the enemy army pursued the retreating Mongols, they stretched their line further into hostile territory. Then the order that He-Who-Goes-First was waiting for came. The call to charge sent the Mongols wielding around and advancing on their pursuers. The enemy had fallen into the trap. Straight Arrow was now behind the first wave. He launched his arrows into the bodies of the enemy field commanders. He-Who-Goes-First was in his usual place at the heart of the battle. His sword and horse were stained with blood as men and body parts littered the ground.

He worked with his ten, and they rushed to the aid of their leader when he was sliced across the back by a broadsword. The men cut down the enemies, and He-Who-Goes-First placed his friend and commander across his horse and once again continued to shred his opponents. The other army was in a state of panic and disarray as they were cut down. They retreated and were pursued by the victorious Mongols. Straight Arrow rushed ahead and caught the battalion commander with an arrow through his throat. The battle continued for several more minutes. It was another decisive victory.

When the dust settled, a figure emerged from the battlefield. It was He-Who-Goes-First carrying the body of his leader of ten. During the ruckus, his horse had been impaled, and the trio fell to the blood soaked earth. He-Who-Goes-First fought on, until he had defeated all who had remained to fight. In the end, his horse was dead, and his friend and leader had left his spirit to ride the wind.

Those who watched saw the warrior walking out of the cloud of dust. His body, armor and clothes were completely covered with the blood of others. He carried the body of his fallen comrade over his shoulder. It was an image that was not unnoticed. The generals of the Khan's army saw He-Who-Goes-First returning from battle with honor. He had behaved admirably when he returned to his ten, and he had sworn allegiance to the new leader. Now, he would be returning to his position as leader of his ten.

Someone else had also noticed. Soonok had returned to the army during the absence of He-Who-Goes-First. His body was scarred from the fire from the sky. His heart was scarred by the hatred of a man who was the son of the man who had killed his father. It was an old wound that had been incurred during another time. It had festered over the years. It did not belong in the new order that the Khan had created, yet it burned inside of him and consumed his soul. They were no longer part of the same ten, but they were still part of the same army. It was something that Soonok could not bear.

He-Who-Goes-First gingerly placed the body he carried at the feet of the generals. He placed the broadsword that had caused his friend's death near their feet as well. He had taken his vengeance on the man who had killed his leader. The sword was proof of his deed. He acknowledged the generals and went to find his son. They had both answered the call to battle bravely this day. While the victory was sweet, He-Who-Goes-First had lost a brother today. He was thankful that he still had a son.

* * * *

The campaign had stretched far. He-Who-Goes-First had never been so far away from the land of his birth before. He saw many strange and wonderful things. He was often glad when they were able to peacefully move through a city. Many would no longer stand against the Khan's army. Yet the further away they got, the harder it was to stay organized and outfitted. They were used to foraging for food and supplies, but they had traveled so far now that each battle seemed to take a larger toll on their stamina.

On those occasions when the soldiers could move about in a strange city, they were able to see the local citizens going about their daily routines. Jenghiz Khan was very interested in the customs of other cultures, and he was continually kept apprised of the wonders of his new empire. Still, his soldiers were not always so welcome. They had to be on guard against assassins or those who may put poison in their food. This was not uncommon, but most of the citizens they met were much too afraid of the consequences if they were discovered.

He-Who-Goes-First had never been schooled, and he was intrigued while in a city that had formal education for its children. This not only meant academics; it also included physical training. This particular city had sophisticated sanitation, which meant that human waste was removed via a network of trenches. Freshwater was also brought in through a separate system. There were even aqueducts for the irrigation of crops.

He watched as artisans pounded metals and created intricate textiles and beadwork. There were musicians and even men who charmed venomous snakes with the sound of their instruments. Straight Arrow accompanied his father around the city, and the two were delighted by the sights and sounds of this wondrous place. It was good that these people were spared from the destruction that so many others had suffered. Perhaps the wisdom and learning of the people here was the reason that they had seen the futility and danger of opposing the Khan.

Such a day as this was a vacation for the soldiers of the Khan's great army. They were able to relax and enjoy themselves. The local population was also interested in the Mongols. They were impressed by the strength and agility of these warriors. Horse races were part of the competition, and He-Who-Goes-First noticed that while the horses of this region were not as round and sturdy as the Mongol ponies, many possessed great speed. He-Who-Goes-First was thrilled by speed. He liked nothing better than to feel a fast horse beneath him, thundering across the ground. It was a feeling like no other.

The Mongols were entitled to tribute in the name of Jenghiz Khan. For sparing this city from death and fire, the Mongols negotiated the price in terms of supplies and some of these fine horses. With a treaty in place, the city and its occupants were now subjects of the Khan's empire. The army left them much as they had been found. Those who were wise enough to cooperate with the Khan's wishes were allowed to live much as they wanted to.

There were times when it was not so easy though. Always there was a city or a king who would send an army against them. When this occurred, the result was a call to battle and the death of many. It was very far from their homeland when the Khan's army found themselves against a very worthy adversary. The soldiers of this army were born of slaves, and they were trained in war from a very early age. They were tough, battle-hardened soldiers who could only gain respect, prestige and power from their exploits in the art of war.

When this army stood before them, the Khan's men recognized the potential danger. Like the wolf that shows respect for the deadly hooves of a large animal, the Mongols knew that this fight would be like no other they had been in. These men were outfitted with the best equipment, and they were literally grown from boys into killers. From across the battlefield, He-Who-Goes-First watched with anticipation as a leader of this force rode a spectacular gray mare in front of his warriors.

He called to his men, and they responded in unison. The dappled gray mare beneath him was breathtaking as it cantered and turned with seemingly little effort from the rider. She crossed the ground with great speed and minimum effort. He-Who-Goes-First was mesmerized by the animal, and he could not take his eyes off of it. Before the day was over, she would be his!

When the battle began, He-Who-Goes-First charged in front of the Khan's army. He headed straight into battle and toward his prize. He was forced to fight through a wall of men before he could get near the man on the gray mare. For the first time in his memory, the Mongols were taking heavy casualties. The toll was very great on both sides as the battle continued. With his ten at the front of the fighting, He-Who-Goes-First lost three men, and two more suffered injuries. Things were not going well, and the call came for the Khan's army to retreat.

As they fought their way backward, He-Who-Goes-First charged through the line once more and flung himself from his mount onto the gray mare and into battle with the fierce man who was riding her. His attack had left the man struggling to regain his balance, and in an instant, they both fell to the ground. The enemy soldier grabbed the throat of He-Who-Goes-First, but the Mongol grabbed his adversary's head with both hands and began to smash it against the trampled and hardened ground. The man's eyes rolled back as his grip loosened. He-Who-Goes-First reached the dagger strapped to his side and plunged it into the man's heart. The whole fight had taken less than a minute, and He-Who-Goes-First grabbed his own horse by the mane and swung onto his back. He chased the gray mare, and amidst the confusion of the battlefield, he was able to grab her reigns.

As the army of the Khan was now in full retreat, He-Who-Goes-First emerged from the fray at full gallop, leading the gray mare away from the fight. The slave army was equally decimated, and they did not pursue their fleeing adversaries. No one could claim a decisive victory, and they were all fully aware that to continue this battle would be disastrous for both sides.

The Mongols continued to ride away to a safe distance. The site of this battle may be the farthest point that they would be able to conquer at this time. They had suffered so many casualties that they would need to replenish their numbers. They had accomplished much on this campaign. They had traveled far into foreign territory. They had conquered many people and many lands in the name of the Khan. Perhaps they had gone as far as they could. There was safety toward home. The distance provided much danger. The generals decided to send word to the Khan of their current state. It would be his decision whether they would continue on or not.

The Khan was a wise man. He would surely make the right decision—whatever that would be. For now, his army tended to their dead and wounded. This battle was over, and neither side was ready to resume fighting. The call to battle had sent many men to the other world. The ground was soaked in blood, and the smell lingered in the nostrils of those who had survived.

Straight Arrow had been slightly wounded by an enemy arrow. His shoulder stung with pain, and it would be a short time before he would be able to regain his sharp-shooting abilities. He-Who-Goes-First had emerged from the battle remarkably well. He suffered only minor cuts and bruises. His ten had been severely depleted. They had been in the worst of the fighting. Never before had they gone against such a worthy army.

Despite the difficulties of this day and the uncertainty of the future, He-Who-Goes-First was busily caring for his horses. He gave extra care to his stallion that had carried him into battle. It had served him well. A warrior was only as great as the horse that carried him. It was the gray mare that he was most intrigued with, however. She was a battle prize. She was still somewhat untrusting of her new surroundings. He-Who-Goes-First was patient, and he continued to talk to her and to stroke her face and neck.

She had calmed down significantly during the few hours that they had been together. She became comfortable with his hands on her. He continued to talk to her, and then he swung himself effortlessly onto her back. She bucked halfheartedly, and then she began to canter across the camp as though she were flying. He kicked her sides, and she began to gallop. She responded to his commands like no horse he had ever known. She could almost sense his thoughts. The other men momentarily stopped their work and watched as the warrior who had become famous for being the first in battle rode his prize around the camp. They nodded appreciatively, for these men knew when a horse and rider were in tune with one another.

Chapter 7:
Horse Sense

The Khan called his army back. He was not willing to lose them stupidly. He knew that they had gone far and that there were limitations to everything. It took a long time for the men, horses and goods to make the long journey back. They were generally excited to return home. Most had families, and those who did not likely would. There would be men who wouldn't return and women who had been made into widows.

He-Who-Goes-First and Straight Arrow returned and greeted Gerka and the daughter of He-Who-Goes-First. She had grown much since they had last seen her. It was a joyful reunion. Straight Arrow was now a man and a soldier. It was only right that he had his own ger. They placed it near the ger of his father and mother. His little sister was still much intrigued with her older brother, and she was overjoyed by the return of her father.

He-Who-Goes-First spent most of his time with his family now. He had been gone for a long time. His life was good. He had missed his wife and daughter very much. He also spent much time with his horses—one in particular. The gray mare was by far his favorite. He took her for rides across the Mongolian Steppe. She was a fantastic animal. She seemed to have much wisdom and strength. Of course her speed was the envy of all the men. Her mottled gray coat also stood out. He-Who-Goes-First kept that coat in perfect condition. He made new armor for her and spent many days getting her used to it.

This was more than just a horse to him. She was possessed with a spirit that shone in her every movement. As experienced as He-Who-Goes-First was at riding, he could scarcely believe the way they seemingly flew across the ground. Her speed was thrilling, and her courage was astounding. She sensed dangers with some extra sensory ability, and she used her speed to escape from it.

He-Who-Goes-First soon learned that to ride this animal, he must let her guide him as much as he would guide her. Working together, they were able to dodge dangers and outmaneuver death. He rode her in battle drills, and she was unmatched by all others. This horse was surely a gift from the spirits.

He-Who-Goes-First took his gray mare hunting, and she was superb at this as well. She won many races and was good in all the games and drills they participated in. In the evenings around the fire, it was agreed that a finer horse could not be found. Many men had offered to buy her, but He-Who-Goes-First would not sell her for any price. On one occasion, he turned down an offer of 40 horses for her.

Soonok had openly rebuked He-Who-Goes-First for turning down such an offer. He said that only a madman would keep one horse when he could have 40. This did not bother He-Who-Goes-First. He had many horses, but none was like this one. She made him happy, and he felt safe riding her. Not even the man who had survived the fire from the sky could sway him to part with her. There had developed a bond between horse and rider that was in a spiritual realm. The horse was simply not for sale at any price.

Over the weeks that they were home, the men of the Khan's army enjoyed themselves very much. When the time came to rejoin the ranks of the army, they were simultaneously sad to leave yet anxious to get back to the work of building an empire. Their new journey took them into lands that they had previously conquered. There had been some rebellion after the Mongols' costly battle with the slave army. In most cases, however, the mere sight of the Khan's army quelled any uprising and brought the leaders of these cities to their senses.

The army continued into new territories, and they eagerly

challenged those who would not yield to the authority of Jenghiz Khan. Inevitably, the day came when they must lay siege to a city whose inhabitants refused to open the gates. As the catapult hurled boulders against the walls, the men waited eagerly for their chance to enter the city. Just before the walls fell, the foreign king opened the gate and begged for leniency. His wish was granted, but the price was high. The Mongols emptied his treasury and sent the contents back to the Khan. The fact that this city remained intact and the inhabitants were allowed to continue living was leniency enough.

When confronted on the battlefield by a fearsome army, the Mongols gladly engaged them. He-Who-Goes-First was always at the front of the fighting. The gray mare beneath him was a blur as she dodged danger and darted in and out of numerous close calls. She was an extra set of eyes for He-Who-Goes-First. She never ceased to amaze him with her instinct and keen senses. He fought hard from her back, and the blood of many men dripped down her sides.

This horse seemed void of the normal fears that many animals had when the smell of death grew strong and the screams of the fallen were ringing in the air. She kept focused on her footing and on the dangers to her and her rider. On more than one occasion, He-Who-Goes-First was sure that she had saved his life.

During one battle, he had felt the wind of a sword coming across his head. He had not seen it coming, yet his horse had sensed the danger and sprung out of the way just in the nick of time. There was another occasion when he kicked her sides to send her running into a fight. She hesitated just long enough for an artillery shot to land in the middle of his destination. The lesson he learned from seeing the boulder land just ahead of his position was not lost on He-Who-Goes-First. He learned to trust his horse's instincts, and he would not reprimand her disobedience. He had found that she would not oppose his will without good reason. This horse had a sense that he could not deny. To do so might be fatal. She had great magic, and he was truly blessed to have such a friend.

It was no mistake whose horse she was. He-Who-Goes-First had only to call her, and she would gallop to him wherever he was. On one particular day, this proved very advantageous. It was during a battle on a very cold day. The fighting had been hard, and He-Who-Goes-First was in the front of it.

Because he was trying to save one of his men who had fallen, He-Who-Goes-First had jumped from his mount and was fighting with his sword on the ground. During the battle, he became separated from the gray mare, and she fell prey to an enemy soldier who wanted to steal her. She fought as the man grabbed her reigns. She stood on her back legs and struck out with her front hooves. Other men joined in, and they were trying to subdue her with ropes. She cried out, and He-Who-Goes-First heard her and called to her. She tried to free herself, but there were four men fighting with her now.

He-Who-Goes-First was occupied in a deadly duel with two men, and he was unable to break free. It was at this moment that another horse crashed through the group of combatants. On his back was Straight Arrow, who was firing his arrows into the men who held the gray mare.

With two of them downed by Straight Arrow, the gray mare kicked one of her captors in the head, and he dropped like a stone beneath her hooves. She pulled free of the other man and charged in the direction of He-Who-Goes-First's voice. He was still fighting, and more men had entered the fray. As the gray mare charged into the middle of the battle, He-Who-Goes-First wrapped an arm around her neck and, at full gallop, swung himself onto her back.

Without even directing her, the horse swung back around, and she carried He-Who-Goes-First back into the fight he had just left. Now on horseback, he swung his sword into the flesh of the enemy soldiers. With his swift mount beneath him, the enemies fell quickly. Straight Arrow was also swinging his sword into the opposing army. In a matter of minutes, the Mongols had once again gained the upper hand. It was the effort of the men and their horses, working together, which won a decisive victory for the Khan that day.

For his continued bravery, the Mongol generals again recognized He-Who-Goes-First. He was raised to the position of leader of 100. Straight Arrow was also recognized. His skill in battle, and particularly with his bow, was quickly helping him to gain rank as well. He was considered to be the very best archer in the Khan's army.

When they weren't in battle, the men spent their time training and telling stories. He-Who-Goes-First had become quite a storyteller, and his ability to put a humorous spin on serious subjects was much appreciated by the other soldiers. Laughter was important to men who experienced so much death and struggle. It was their outlet to an otherwise brutal existence. They spent long hours in the evenings, drinking kumiss and listening and laughing at the stories He-Who-Goes-First would tell.

Always absent from these friendly gatherings was the man Soonok. He continued to despise the new leader of 100. He was no longer open about his hatred. He kept it buried deep within his black heart for fear that his hatred would inspire hostility against himself. He-Who-Goes-First was a popular soldier and leader. Most of the men did not want to hear others talking ill of him.

Chapter 8:
The Right Fit

He-Who-Goes-First was soon at odds with himself over his new position. As leader of 100, he had gained prestige, yet this new position troubled him. He was no longer able to ride up front, headlong into battle. His new duties required him to stay behind the front line and direct his ten leaders of ten. It was not so bad, he thought. There was less danger of being killed or injured. Still, he wanted to kick his horse's ribs and ride her into the middle of the fight. After the first battle this way, he decided to talk with the generals and explain his reluctance to continue on as leader of 100.

As he spoke, the generals nodded in appreciation. They had noticed his demeanor had changed with the last battle, and they knew that he was not happy behind the skirmish line. Perhaps someday this would do, but not right now. He-Who-Goes-First was still young, and he was an excellent combat soldier. They granted him leave from his new position.

Then one of the generals presented a new idea. Perhaps there were more options than just returning to his position as leader of ten. There were other opportunities for a warrior like He-Who-Goes-First. The general asked him if he was interested in artillery. He didn't think so. How about diplomacy? This definitely did not interest him. Then the general brought up reconnaissance. This was something that He-Who-Goes-First *was* interested in.

It was decided that He-Who-Goes-First would accompany a small group of men experienced in reconnaissance on their next mission. In fact, they had a mission that very night. He was sent to be briefed by the leader of the team. He was a well-known warrior who was highly respected. The mission would be undertaken by only three men. Stealth was the key to such an expedition, and the fewer men there were, the less was the likelihood of being discovered while infiltrating enemy lines.

The men of recon routinely napped in the afternoon, and they frequently left the camp in the middle of the night. They were so quiet that the sentries were often hard-pressed to notice them. Upon returning to the camp before first light, they used a variety of signals to warn the sentries of their approach, so to avoid a confrontation with their own forces.

He-Who-Goes-First settled in for his nap late in the afternoon. He had some difficulty falling asleep and was roused sometime later by the recon leader, Tousan. They mounted their horses and rode out of the camp. Tousan led the way as they moved across the dark landscape in the direction of the next conquest. He-Who-Goes-First was disoriented in the darkness, but Tousan and the other man, Akeel, seemed to be keenly aware of where they were going.

Finally, Tousan motioned for the men to dismount. They left their horses under the cover of some scrub bushes and began to move forward on foot. It was slow going, as the moon was only a sliver of light in the night sky. The men who led He-Who-Goes-First brought him over obstacles and kept low to the ground. Tousan pointed, and up ahead, He-Who-Goes-First could faintly make out the image of a man. As they watched, the outlines of other men were coming into view. They had horses, and periodically the muted sound of one of the animals was carried in the direction of the Mongols.

On this night, they were simply assessing the strength of this force. It was not a particularly impressive group—a few hundred men and horses. The next day, the Mongols would ride through them and scatter them like the wind. Their job was done, and they began to move quietly back to where they had hidden their horses. Before they reached this destination, Akeel stopped and nodded to Tousan. Then he held up four fingers and motioned to He-Who-Goes-First to arm his bow.

Ahead of them were their three horses. Behind the horses were at least four scouts from the army they had just seen. They had run into their counterparts from the enemy force, who were now waiting in ambush for them. Akeel motioned for He-Who-Goes-First to follow him. They went to the right, while Tousan went to the left. Each man crawled on his belly through the darkness, knowing that the enemy was watching for them. Slowly they worked themselves onto either side of their quarry. A faint sound came from Tousan's position, and Akeel and He-Who-Goes-First sat up and took aim. All at once, there was screaming and confusion as the arrows sailed at the men waiting in ambush. They returned fire—those who could—and the three Mongols charged them and finished the enemies with their swords.

The quiet had been shattered, and they could hear the shouts of the men from the enemy camp. The Mongols jumped onto their horses and made their exit into the night. Riding at full gallop was treacherous in the dark, and they soon slowed their pace when it was evident that the enemy was not in pursuit. They made their way back to the Mongol camp, and Tousan opened his mouth and made a sound undistinguishable from that of a golden eagle. Satisfied, their sentries let them ride into the camp.

The generals were awakened with the news of what had happened. They nodded and announced their intent to attack immediately. The sun was still sometime off from rising in the eastern sky, but this was the time to move. The men of the camp rose quickly and prepared themselves for battle.

There were many times in the past when He-Who-Goes-First had been awakened to a similar situation, but never before did he have the insight as to what had actually provoked it. The next day, the story would circulate. But as it made its way from man to man, inevitably the story would undergo many changes from what had actually taken place.

As he made ready to return to the enemy position, He-Who-Goes-First noticed that Straight Arrow was at his side. His son was curious about what had happened.

"We found them," his father answered. "Their scouts found our horses and were waiting for us when we came back. They are dead now, and we are going to finish the rest of them. It will not be their day."

Straight Arrow nodded, and they mounted up and rode into the night. When they arrived near the enemy camp, things had quieted, but there was a heightened sense of awareness. There was no reason to be stealthy, so the Mongols charged the camp with swords drawn and firebrands blazing. Straight Arrow and a group of archers were shooting flaming arrows into the camp, and the enemy soldiers were terrified as they ran in all directions.

As promised, the Mongols literally rode through the camp. They did not bother to pursue such a pathetic force and only killed those who were easily accessible. They gathered the horses and supplies of the vanquished army, burned all that was left and continued forward.

He-Who-Goes-First was exhilarated by all he had been witness to. He had been involved in every stage of this maneuver. He had scouted the enemy and had still been free to charge headlong into their camp when the battle began. Perhaps reconnaissance was something that he would enjoy. He had much to learn, but it was a new challenge for him. Perhaps it was the right fit for him at this time.

After traveling for several hours, the Mongols arrived outside of a great city. As the sun was now in the west side of the sky, the generals called the three members of the previous night's recon team—plus one more. Straight Arrow was given the order to join them. On this night, they would infiltrate the city. They would need a marksman of uncanny ability. This would be a dangerous mission.

Father and son were pleased to be working together. Once again, Tousan would be at the lead, and Akeel would be second. They had gladly accepted He-Who-Goes-First and his son. Theirs was an elite order, but this man and his son had proven themselves on many occasions. But before the sun sank below the horizon, they had to sleep.

Once again, He-Who-Goes-First was woken up by the leader

Tousan. When they met Akeel, he was already waiting with Straight Arrow. They started out again on horseback. They left their horses in a hiding place and made their way on foot to their destination. There was very little cover as they approached the walls of the sleeping city. There were sentries posted, and it would be difficult to infiltrate. Akeel went ahead with Straight Arrow as Tousan and He-Who-Goes-First waited in the shadows.

It took a while for the two men to quietly move up near the wall and the single sentry located above that corner. He-Who-Goes-First could not see his two comrades who had disappeared up ahead. Suddenly, the sentry fell from sight. Tousan and He-Who-Goes-First knew that it was the result of an expertly shot arrow. They reached the other two men and formed a human ladder with their bodies. Straight Arrow was the smallest, so he was first to climb to the top and pull himself over the wall. He wedged himself tightly in place as the other men began to climb, using his body to pull themselves up.

One look at the fallen sentry showed the efficiency of his demise. An arrow had opened a hole in his throat. When he had fallen, he no longer possessed the ability to cry out. So far, they had made it over the wall undetected. Tousan led as the team continued on. They were soon at work examining the structure of the wall and deciding how it could best be circumvented. Tousan went alone into the city while the others secured the gate by killing the two guards who were watching it.

The guards had grown sleepy, and only one was awake when the arrow buried itself into the back of his skull. He lay on the hard ground twitching as Akeel cut the throat of the other guard as he slept. He-Who-Goes-First quietly unlatched the gate, and then they went to find out where the horses of this city were stabled. While much of the fodder was grown on the outside of the city, it was in fact an enormous place. There were gardens and a large area to pasture horses and livestock within the walls.

When they found the horses, Tousan was already waiting. The animals were becoming alarmed, and the Mongols decided to act quickly. They jumped onto some of the horses and created a stampede, which they directed toward the gate that was still closed, but unsecured. They rode up and swung open the massive gate, as the sentries (from the far side) who were still left sounded the alarm. The recon team charged out of the city and back to their own horses. They reclaimed their own animals and continued back to the Mongol encampment with as many stolen horses as they could keep together.

On the following morning, the Khan's army moved on the city. Word came from a messenger who had come from behind the walls that the gates would be opened without resistance. The population was sufficiently terrified by the Khan's army and what had happened the night before. There was no battle that day, simply a show of force.

He-Who-Goes-First continued on with his duties in reconnaissance. Eventually, he learned this skill very well. He became confident in his abilities to move unheard and unseen in the dark of night. At times, he was even sent out alone into hostile territory. Most often, he still worked with Tousan and Akeel. When they needed an expert archer, they also brought Straight Arrow.

Reconnaissance seemed to be the right fit for He-Who-Goes-First. He had wanted a new challenge, and this was affording him the excitement that he craved. On one night, he went alone into a kingdom and, in the darkness, attempted to blend in, disguised as a local citizen. He was gaining valuable information as he walked through the city, until he was met by a group of soldiers on patrol. They asked him something in a language he did not understand. As they surrounded him, he was forced to surrender or they would have killed him.

He was beaten, though he would not have talked even if he had understood them. Then he was placed under guard in a cell. He was sure that his execution was forthcoming. As luck would have it, he soon heard the sounds of battle growing closer as the Khan's army laid siege to this city. One of his captors decided to expedite the execution and came into the cell with his sword.

When things were hopeless, He-Who-Goes-First was at his most dangerous. He pretended to beg for his life as he kneeled on the floor with his arms over his head. When the man swung his sword,

He-Who-Goes-First rolled out of the way and jumped to his feet. As the other man tried to recover from the swing he had missed with the sword, the Mongol warrior kicked his would-be executioner, and the man dropped to the floor reaching for his injured testicles.

He-Who-Goes-First picked up the man's sword, and after permanently ending his adversary's pain, he joined the fighting that was entering the city. The men who had beaten him were unfortunate enough to find the newly liberated warrior behind them as they attempted to fend off an assault by the Mongol army to their front.

Though he still hurt from his beatings, He-Who-Goes-First dispatched these men with great relish. The city was now burning, and the Khan's force was again victorious. As He-Who-Goes-First watched the fires burn, Straight Arrow appeared and was overjoyed to see his father still alive. That night, they discussed the pros and cons of recon work. There was a safety within the mass of highly trained soldiers that was absent on many reconnaissance missions. As skilled as a man might be, he could not always defeat a group of armed men on his own. Still, this was the first really close call that He-Who-Goes-First had since beginning his new occupation. It was dangerous to be a soldier, regardless of your duties.

Chapter 9:
Know Thy Enemy

    Something rather peculiar happened one night while He-Who-Goes First was on a routine recon patrol. He was once again by himself, and he was far from his camp, face-to-face with a member of the enemy force he had been sent to spy on. The other man had been sent to do reconnaissance on the Mongol army. In a way, the two men were nearly looking at a reflection of themselves as they stared into each other's eyes.

    It so happened that these two men understood each other's language, and by some twist of fate, they began a conversation out there in "no man's land"—halfway between their respective armies. Each stood a few feet from the other and tried to size up his adversary.

    It was not unheard of in times of war that men from opposing sides would sometimes have occasion to stop fighting long enough to get acquainted. It made for an interesting situation, since it was more difficult to kill someone you knew and recognized as a fellow human being than it was to kill an enemy stranger. Still, these men were on opposite sides of a political battle that was larger than each of them—or both of them.

    Neither man was quite sure what to do as they asked and evaded questions of each other. He-Who-Goes-First found the man to be interesting, and the other soldier found the Mongol to be in possession of a rather likeable wit. At the moment, there was no pressing need to act, and from all appearances, each was working alone on this night. They continued to talk, and soon the conversation turned to their rather unique situation.

They queried each other over how this situation should be resolved. They could both turn and walk away and return to their respective camps. This would require an explanation when their superiors were not in receipt of any intelligence information. The actual truth of the situation was not likely to win any approval from a listening general either. There was also the option of fighting to the death. This was not the most attractive idea now, since they had become acquainted.

Had they been born under the same banner, they may have grown up to be friends. This was a prospect that was not helping to remedy the current situation. To avoid the inevitable, they began trading stories about family and friends. Each was careful not to spill any military secrets to the other, though the conversation became more engaging. How much longer could this continue? Neither was certain how long they had been involved in this predicament, but they had both continued longer than either thought to be wise.

What if more men showed up from the other side? What if they did choose to walk away from this battle and one or the other shot his adversary in the back? What if they were found out when they returned and were accused of treason? This was becoming quite a bit more complicated than either man had ever hoped for. It was certain that neither could allow the other to continue his mission without a fight.

As the night continued on, they began discussing their options with more desperation. It was their duty to get information about the enemy and to return to camp. If confronted, they were under orders to escape by any means necessary. It was also their duty to prevent the other from returning to his own force with any intelligence about the other side. Obviously they had both made a serious mistake by not immediately trying to kill each other.

That was what they had to do, they decided. They would fight a duel to the death. As they realized what this decision meant, neither was prepared to make the first move. Both were comfortable in engaging in battle, if the other initiated it. As they stood staring at each other, neither man lifted his sword or made a move toward the other.

Perhaps this was not the way things would go after all. Finally, with great difficulty, they made an agreement which bound each one by his honor as a man and as a soldier. They would each back away and return to their own camp without completing the mission that they had been commissioned to do that night. They bid each other farewell, and both backed away from the other into the darkness of the night.

He-Who-Goes-First returned to his camp without the knowledge that he had been sent to retrieve. He made no lengthy explanations to the generals of his army. He simply said that he was unable to retrieve the information they had wanted, without risking detection and possible capture or death. This was not exactly an adequate explanation in the eyes of the generals, and they let He-Who-Goes-First know that he had failed them. He would be returning to his duties as a leader of ten.

He-Who-Goes-First nodded and accepted this decision. His experience had caused him to doubt his own worthiness as a reconnaissance scout. Would not Tousan or Akeel have gone directly into battle with the enemy soldier? He was certain that they would have. Still, he felt that there was some lesson to be learned from what had happened to him. He did not know what it was exactly, nor was he sure how it could change his destiny in this life.

As he thought about all that had happened, he noticed a shadow pass over him in the morning sky. It was an eagle sailing on the wind above. As he watched it fly, he remembered his boyhood and how he liked to watch the eagles when he was the guardian of horses. The bird gave him renewed resolve, and he accepted what he had done and where his actions had now taken him.

By afternoon, the Mongol army stood across from their next opponents. The foreign army was poised and ready for the assault. The Mongols were waiting for the battle cry. When the orders came, He-Who-Goes-First charged ahead, as was his custom. He led his ten into battle in the name of the Khan. Somewhere amidst the fighting and bloodshed, his eyes locked with those of another man from the enemy army. It was the man he had met during the night. They had spared each other their swords less than a day before, and as fate would have it, they met again in the middle of a huge clash of warriors from both sides. Apparently they had unfinished business and an unfinished fight. The spirits were not going to let them off the hook so easy.

They rode their horses close, and then they each got down from their mounts. They faced each other, swords in hand just as they had before. As the eagle soared above them, the clank of metal could be heard as they finished their fight that they had seemingly only postponed just hours before. They fought without words or emotion. It was only destiny and duty that pushed them on. Each was a worthy opponent, and their private battle continued as those around them waged a different war.

* * * *

He-Who-Goes-First emerged from the battle. The fighting was not quite over yet, but his battle had ended. His opponent lay on the battlefield. His blood soaked into the parched earth as his spirit left his body to ride on the wind. Another enemy soldier rode at He-Who-Goes-First, who swung his sword and sidestepped, stabbing the man through the eye without so much as a second look. The man dropped from his mount, and He-Who-Goes-First continued to walk away from the now almost finished battle.

He had done his duty. This was a day he would not soon forget. Somehow, the battle had changed for him. There was a battle raging in his soul as he led the gray mare away from the blood of the enemy he had come to know and finally killed.

* * * *

He-Who-Goes-First sat quietly cleaning and sharpening his weapons. The battleaxe he was working on was still soiled from war. The brain tissue he cleaned off of it was likely from the man he had been forced to kill…even after they had the chance to meet and talk. This thought was troubling to him. He could accept that he had done what he had to do, yet it was unsettling for him. Was the other man perhaps the spiritual victor, since he did not have to suffer from these thoughts?

Never before had He-Who-Goes-First doubted his mission, his occupation or his Khan. Now, he had been forced to see a reflection of himself in the eyes of another man. Neither of them was either good nor bad. They were simply following the orders of those who outranked them. He knew that it could have been he who had died, and in some ways, he longed for that peace. It was all quite unsettling for a warrior who had sent many men to the other world. This was something that could ruin him as a soldier in the Khan's army. He would have to somehow get past these thoughts…this…guilt!

Straight Arrow sat near, working on his bows. One was lighter for short range, and the other was a heavy weapon that was used for distance. He was restringing his lighter weapon, which had sustained some damage in the last battle. Straight Arrow knew that something about that battle and the previous night was weighing heavily on the mind of his father. He was not sure exactly what it was or if it was appropriate for him to ask about it. For the moment, he stayed close by and silently worked on his bow.

He-Who-Goes-First cleaned the last of the dried brain tissue from his axe. He took his sharpening stone and began to put a new edge on the weapon. The battle between him and the man he had come to know had become very close and personal. Each man had tried to kill the other, though it was not what either had wanted. In the end, as they rolled on the ground, it was He-Who-Goes-First who applied the edge of his battleaxe to the head of his opponent. It was not a quick death, since both men were wearing armor, which included helmets made of metal and leather. Essentially, He-Who-Goes-First had chopped through his opponent's helmet and ultimately his head with a series of blows from the axe.

He had witnessed many brutal killings. Many of them were by his own hand. It wasn't until this moment, however, that he had any doubt that it was anything less than an honorable undertaking. He was not an educated man, though he was wise in many ways. He was sure that the man he had killed would be reborn into a new person one day. This knowledge had always been a comfort to him when he was confronted with the death of a friend or family member. It was also one of the reasons that he could risk his life time after time in battle. After meeting the man in "no man's land," and forming a temporary truce with him, something inside of He-Who-Goes-First had changed.

It was essential that he should will himself beyond this inner struggle. If he could not, he would be of no use to the Khan or his brothers in battle. He would either have to leave the army in disgrace, or he would almost certainly die at the hand of another enemy soldier.

What did it really mean when your spirit left you to ride upon the wind? He remembered the near death experience that he had had. He rubbed the back of his head unconsciously and then realized what he was doing when he felt the knot in his skull where he had been injured.

He finished sharpening his axe and then began to apply a lacquer made from fish to his shield. As he worked it into the leather, he continued to ponder the ideas of life and death. It was, after all, the right of the Khan to decide whether a battle was just or not. He-Who-Goes-First should not be having such thoughts as these, as they were nothing less than treason. Still, he understood that he was an individual, and as a singular being, he had some opportunity to exercise free will. Or did he? He was merely one of many soldiers in the Khan's army. Each was bound by his honor to fulfill his duty to the empire of Temuchin.

He laid his shield out next to him to dry. The weather was becoming cold, and the lacquer would freeze-dry quickly. He checked both of his bows and was satisfied that they were in good repair. He pulled out his sword and ran a finger along the curved blade. It could use a new edge. He cleaned the dried blood from it and began to apply his stone to sharpen it. Perhaps, he thought, he himself was not unlike the sword or the battleaxe. Maybe he had just lost his edge. If he could only find out how to sharpen his will and determination, he would once again know that he was among the best of the Khan's warriors.

Any man could crack under the strain of continuous combat. He was no weakling, however, in either mind or body. Straight Arrow finally asked him if he was ill. He-Who-Goes-First answered that his mind was "full," and he was trying to make sense of his life. Straight Arrow was relieved that his father was not physically sick, but he sensed that the battle he now fought within his mind was just as serious.

As he continued to sharpen his sword, He-Who-Goes-First thought about the idea of free will verses following orders. At what point should a man subscribe to either policy? If he had let the other man live, and that man had killed one of the Khan's soldiers, would not the blood of his brother be on his hands as well? His spirit was damaged but not broken. He knew that the empire that they were building for the Khan was an honorable venture. There were laws now, and those who accepted the rule of Jenghiz Khan lived in a world that was relatively safe. Certainly his own people, the people of the steppe, were better off now that they were no longer stealing animals and killing each other in the perennial raids that had previously existed between different bands. Now they were all one people, under the Khan.

Over the next few days, He-Who-Goes-First became more resolved with his place in the world. He was loyal to his Khan, and life was good for his people under Temuchin's leadership. It was the duty of every soldier to bring these ideals to the lands they conquered, whether it was through a peaceful transition or through military conquest. As a member of the Khan's army, it was his job to enforce the will of his leader through military might.

The death of the man he had come to know on that last reconnaissance mission, though regrettable, was unavoidable. It was not his place to question the natural order of things. If the spirits had wanted things to be different, they most certainly would have been. If he was meant to die in the name of the Khan, that too would have been.

He had repaired his weapons and, for the most part, his soul. Inside of him, there would still be some doubt that would linger. He had, however, closed it behind a door in his mind that he dared not open. He had to remain sharp and focused—like a well kept sword. He had to maintain his edge if he was to continue to serve the Khan and fight well with his brothers.

Soon after, Straight Arrow noticed that his father had regained his sense of humor. He knew that there was a dark force inside of the man that had to be wrestled with periodically, as one would wrestle any opponent. He was glad to see that He-Who-Goes-First had won this battle. He would have expected no less. Soon, they would be back on the battlefield, and all would be as it should be.

Chapter 10: The Edge

A sword that develops a dull edge is inferior in battle to one that is kept sharp. This is also the case with men. When the time came for He-Who-Goes-First to take up his sword and ride into battle, he did so with the same skill and determination that he always had. He had worked on his mind and conquered his doubts. He was as sharp as his sword as he rode in front of his ten while they tested the enemy in battle. Beneath him, his gray mare performed as well as his sword as they defied all attempts to stop them.

While the main force of the Mongols advanced into the lines of their opposition, others of the Khan's army moved around their quarry from the outside. In only minutes, the enemy soldiers were surrounded, and there was no means of escape. The generals watched and nodded in appreciation as their troops worked. The organization was incredible to see.

He-Who-Goes-First was involved in a frontal assault, while his son Straight Arrow was among those who enveloped the enemy. As the fighting continued, the smell of blood permeated the air as it soaked into the snow of the frozen battlefield. The world had been bright white that morning, and now the snow was splattered red, as Mars grinned down at the Earth. The air was filled with steam from men, horses and gaping wounds. Blood spilled warm and steamed in great puddles beneath the combatants' feet. Here and there, patches of white remained, though the battlefield had been discolored and trampled by men and horses.

He-Who-Goes-First was working with his sword, as he preferred to do in such close proximity. His ten stayed near to each other. They seemed to have eyes that looked to the rear as well as to the front. Those things that they did not see for themselves were seen by others of the ten. It was not uncommon for each man to both save another and be saved from a blow himself, over and over within the same battle.

Organized by the decimal system, both communications and help came in tens and hundreds. During the battle, He-Who-Goes-First noticed that the neighboring ten was surrounded by enemy soldiers. With a yell, he kicked the gray mare, and his ten crashed through the fighting and freed their brothers from one side of the struggle. With this type of cooperation, the battle was soon over, and the enemy was decisively defeated.

As the battlefield steamed red, the Mongols returned to their ranks. It was then that He-Who-Goes-First noticed the blood trickling down his leg. He had been hit by a sword and had not noticed it during the height of the battle. The wound was not bad. The silk undergarments that the Mongols wore were strong. While his skin had been broken, the strength of the silk had not been penetrated by the glancing blow. This had diminished the severity of the wound, and had also kept the dirt of the battlefield from entering into it.

He laughed as he was treated, and in typical style, he made a joke about the condition of the man who had done this to him. One of his ten agreed and said that it was he who had sent that man's spirit to the wind. He-Who-Goes-First laughed heartily and nodded. They had all fought well. Each man was as sharp as his sword, and together they possessed an edge that was unmatched by any other army.

That evening, as they ate and drank Kumiss, He-Who-Goes-First entertained those who sat with him. He told a story that was loosely based on a dream that he'd had.

"A man and his horse were traveling in a foreign land when they came upon a golden eagle with an injured wing. The eagle had the power of human speech, so he asked the man to stop and help him. The man was not sure if he should trust the eagle, but they continued talking until he was persuaded to come down from his horse and look at the injured bird's wing. When the man held the wing out to examine it, there was no visible damage. He asked the eagle how it was that he had been injured. The eagle said that he would have to show the man. He told the man to place the eagle on top of his head, and he would demonstrate how his wing had been damaged. The man did as he was asked, and the eagle quickly plucked out both of his eyes and devoured them.

"The man screamed in pain and asked why the eagle had done such a thing. The bird answered that now that he had eaten the man's eyes, he had the power to see great distances. The eagle flew away, and indeed, his vision had become quite acute.

"The man was now blind, and he found his horse, but he did not know where he was going, so they fell into a ravine during the night when neither could see. The horse had been killed by the fall, and the man ate the animal and used its skin to keep warm for the whole of the winter until spring arrived. When the rains came, the ravine filled with water, and the man drowned. When he awoke, he found himself emerging from the water with a new set of eyes, since he was being born into the life of a new baby boy.

"The boy grew up and became a man. One day, he was climbing a large rock when he found the eagle who had taken his eyes. The bird was very old, and he could no longer fly. The man asked the eagle if he had very good vision. The eagle replied that he did have excellent vision in his youth, but it was not so good anymore. The man asked him if he had ever broken his wing. The eagle suddenly recognized the man, and he began to plead for his life. The man said that he would not take the eyes of the eagle. Instead, he pulled the wings off of the bird, and he attached them to his own back with a length of sinew.

"Then he jumped from the top of the rock, and though he flapped the wings as hard as he could, he fell to the earth below and lay broken but still alive.

"'Why could I not fly?' he called up to the eagle with no wings.

"'You should have eaten them!' the bird replied.

"'Would that have made me fly?' he asked.

"'No,' replied the eagle, 'but at least you wouldn't have fallen to your death!'"

The other men chuckled and nodded in approval. They had come to enjoy these stories which became funnier as they continued to drink Kumiss. The camaraderie was enjoyed by all except for one man. Soonok sat beyond the light of the fire. He ran his hand over the scar tissue that had covered his body where he had been burned by the fire from the sky. His burns had healed into scars, but the scar in his heart still burned hot. He would never be happy until he saw He-Who-Goes-First dead. He had dedicated his life to it. He only needed the right opportunity to strike. He only needed an edge.

* * * *

The weather continued to get colder as winter gained the upper hand. The Khan recalled his army before they became stranded far from home. As they traveled back to the steppes of Mongolia, they made a few stops at some of the cities and kingdoms they had previously conquered. The Khan liked to reinforce his dominance over some of the more rebellious of his subjects. It sent a strong message when the Khan's army came by to visit your town.

Recently, He-Who-Goes-First had been selected as one of the bodyguards who accompanied the diplomatic envoy that entered the opened gates on such visits. He stood with his ten as the diplomats exchanged greetings and messages with the leadership. He-Who-Goes-First was frequently unable to understand the language of the exchange. His job was simply to supply an intimidating presence. If there was any kind of dispute, there were thousands more just like him waiting on the outside.

It was interesting to enter these foreign cities, and He-Who-Goes-First kept a keen eye on all that went on around him. His position on these ventures also sometimes afforded him a chance to spend a short time inside the relative warmth of a palace or other indoor meeting place. On occasion, he may even be offered food or drink. He had accepted such offerings from time to time, but he remained aware that the chance always existed that these gifts could contain poisons. Usually he refused such hospitality and kept his attention on the business at hand.

There were times when he felt secure and others when he knew the chance for trouble was only a breath away. His instincts were usually good in these types of situations. Even if the leader of a particular place cooperated with the Khan, it was possible that others in the immediate area might feel differently. Generally speaking, coming under the domination of the Khan was not something that most of these people had originally wanted. Most often, such a state of affairs was thrust upon them, since to defy Temuchin was almost without fail a fatal mistake.

There were times when the conversation between the diplomats became heated. If the situation persisted, He Who Goes First and his men would step forward with their swords drawn, and order was almost always immediately restored. On one particular occasion, however, the situation became unhinged.

The ruler of the small kingdom they had entered was openly resentful of their presence. He had recently gained power after the death of his father. Subjugation of the kingdom had occurred during his father's rule, and the new king was young and brash. His inexperience caused him to fail to afford the Khan's envoy the respect that he should have. He spoke belligerently, believing that he was secure in the presence of his bodyguards who were well-armed, enormous men.

As the situation grew increasingly tense, He-Who-Goes-First and his ten stepped forward with their swords drawn. The young king's bodyguards reciprocated, and the boldness of the young ruler was intensified. Within these close quarters, his forces appeared to have the upper hand. The Khan's army was assembled outside, however, and unbeknownst to the boy king, his actions were jeopardizing everything that he was the ruler of.

Finally, the young man had had enough, and he ordered his men to kill the intruders who had insulted his position. The room erupted as the guards moved on the Mongols. The insolent young king was among the first to fall. He-Who-Goes-First and his ten shoved the Khan's diplomats out of harm's way and engaged the enemy in battle. Tables were overturned, and blood spilled on the floor as the swift and blinding violence reached its peak.

While the royal guards were large and strong, they lacked the experience, speed and determination of the smaller band of nomads. The Khan's warriors tore through the guards like a pack of wolves on a struggling fawn. They lashed out with swords, and the severed limbs of their adversaries fell to the floor. The entire room was splattered with blood, and all were dead within moments—except for the Mongol warriors. None was killed, and only one was injured. The cut was not serious, and they fought their way out of the room and into the square outside.

The call went out by tens, hundreds and thousands, and the Khan's army quickly pushed through the gate with amazing speed. The inhabitants were terrified! The sister of the fallen boy king pleaded for mercy for her kingdom. She offered to give in to all the Khan's demands if they would only spare the kingdom. She asked that the actions of her dead brother not be held against the rest of the Khan's "loyal subjects."

The order was given for the army to stand down. The diplomat arranged a deal that he was sure would be acceptable to the Khan. If this princess would agree to accompany the Mongols back to their Khan, she could present herself before Jenghiz himself and the kingdom would be spared. Reluctantly, the young woman agreed, and she quickly assembled a contingent of servants to accompany her.

The Mongol army returned to their journey homeward, leaving behind the shattered peace of a small kingdom that was in need of another new ruler. The mistake that had been made that day was still visible among the dead bodies and splattered blood that littered the royal hall. The events of this day would not be forgotten anytime soon. Those who remained knew that they had narrowly escaped certain death but for the selfless act of one young woman who was now riding away to become one of the wives of the barbarian emperor known as Jenghiz Khan.

He-Who-Goes-First rode forward with the other soldiers. He had regained his edge in mind and body. No longer did he battle with himself over right and wrong. The young king had made a mistake. It was no different than an animal who gave in to fear as the eagle flew over. If it remained still, it might be unseen and live for another day. If it became frightened and ran, the eagle would fall upon it, and it would be devoured. The young man had become unglued during his dialogue with the Khan's diplomats. His actions led to his death. Such was the way life was for all. One must maintain his edge if he hoped to see the sun rise tomorrow.

Chapter 11:
All the Way Home

Winter enveloped the steppe as the soldiers returned to their families. Gerka was pleased to have her family back. Though her husband was gone for months or sometimes years at a time, she still felt lucky that he had not wanted more than one wife. He sometimes joked that one was "more than enough!!!" He usually embraced her when he said this so that there was no mistaking how he really felt.

The life of a soldier's wife was filled with loneliness; but when he was around, Gerka had the full attention of her husband. That was, except for the fact that he was spending much of his time with their daughter as well. He-Who-Goes-First marveled at how quickly the child was growing. The little girl brought him much joy as he told her stories and took her for walks with her dog.

Straight Arrow had taken up residence with his new wife. She was older than he, which was common in their culture. She had been widowed and already had a young son. The child of a Mongol's wife was also the child of her husband. Spiritual bonds were stronger than those of the flesh. Straight Arrow might still be a young man, but he proved to be a devoted father, willing to share his knowledge and skills with his new son.

The cold of the winter was offset by the warmth of family life. There was sufficient food, and the time passed quickly. However, never could life be so simple as to not provide new challenges for the nomads. During the height of the winter's reign, a sickness spread throughout the village encampment. Those who were taken ill suffered from chills and sweats. They had respiratory problems and were prone to diarrhea and vomiting.

It was the onset of influenza, which was not uncommon at this time of the year. It was particularly hard on those who were very young or very old. The village lost several infants and young children before the epidemic subsided. Straight Arrow's son was taken ill, and he and his wife spent many nights awake while the boy suffered. For a time, they were not sure if he would recover. The healer had come to visit, but he was kept very busy by the epidemic. In the end, even this man of medicine was taken ill. Nearly everyone was sick for at least a day or two.

He-Who-Goes-First spent two days ill. He thought he might not be affected when he remained healthy during his wife and daughter's bout with it. Just about the time they started feeling better, however, he also became ill. The illness was hard on the community, and He-Who-Goes-First was glad that there was no enemy to fight off. In the old days, feuds between neighboring clans were frequent, and such a widespread sickness would leave the village open to an attack. Under the rule of the mighty Khan, such infighting was nearly extinguished. Only on rare occasions was there a problem of this nature.

There were still a few who clung to the old ways and the old hatreds. Soonok lived in a neighboring village, and he had heard that the village of He-Who-Goes-First had been hit hard by the influenza. His own community had several cases, but they were far fewer in number. Soonok decided that he would visit the village of He-Who-Goes-First and see if his nemesis had been taken ill.

He-Who-Goes-First was starting to feel better, and he had ventured outside of the ger to get some much needed exercise. As he walked to the edge of his village, he was approached by the man Soonok. Soonok called out to He-Who-Goes-First and began to try to provoke an altercation. He-Who-Goes-First asked Soonok what business he had in the village. Soonok replied by making a disparaging remark about Gerka. Though he was still feeling weak, He-Who-Goes-First was in no mood to have someone insult his beloved wife.

Soonok persisted. He-Who-Goes-First asked him to leave and

also told the man that he did not care to fight him. Soonok smiled and asked if the son of the man who had killed his father had become a coward.

"The son of the man who killed your father?" repeated He-Who-Goes-First.

So that was it! This was the reason that this man had developed such a hatred for He-Who-Goes-First. The grudge was left over from the days of long ago. Again, He-Who-Goes-First told Soonok that he would derive no pleasure from continuing a fight that their fathers had started many years before. Soonok stepped forward with his battleaxe, and suddenly, He-Who-Goes-First realized that he had left his ger without bothering to arm himself.

As Soonok rushed forward, He-Who-Goes-First moved to dodge the attack and realized that the aftermath of his illness had left him weak and dizzy. At that moment, the dog that his daughter had become so fond of came to the aid of the leader of his pack. The animal was not large, but neither was it small. It launched itself at the intruder and sunk its teeth into the man's leg. It twisted and shook as it tried to knock its victim from his feet. Soonok screamed in pain and raised the battleaxe to strike the dog. Before he could bring the weapon down, He-Who-Goes-First grabbed his arm, and though his body had been weakened, his will was strong. He forced the arm of Soonok behind his back, and he heard something snap.

Soonok now realized that he was not going to win this battle. His arm had gone numb and his fingers let the axe fall harmlessly to the ground. He-Who-Goes-First pulled his daughter's dog away from the defeated man and told Soonok to leave while he still could. Soonok limped to his horse and climbed onto its back. He glared back at He-Who-Goes-First, who was still holding the growling and bristling canine. Straight Arrow appeared just in time to see the man and horse gallop away.

"He had come to kill me," He-Who-Goes-First told his son. "He thought he had an edge."

Straight Arrow half grunted his reply, "Looks like he was mistaken."

They laughed halfheartedly, and He-Who-Goes-First went to find a piece of meat or a bone for the dog. His daughter's best friend was a worthy warrior. He had come to the aid of one of his family without any consideration for his own safety. From that day forward, He-Who-Goes-First would refer to the dog as "Edge."

Straight Arrow was troubled by what had happened. The man Soonok obviously held some grudge against his father. It was one thing to face your enemy on the battlefield and quite another to have someone in your own army who wanted to see you dead. He vowed to keep one eye on his father and the other on the man who wore the scars from the fire from the sky. He was sure this was not yet over.

The remainder of the winter was less eventful. The son of Straight Arrow and his wife recovered from his illness. His father made for him a child-sized bow and arrows. He-Who-Goes-First continued to enjoy his time with his wife and daughter. As spring approached, the soldiers began training for battle. They raced their horses, which was a favorite pastime of He-Who-Goes-First. There was still no other horse that could beat his beloved gray mare. He also enjoyed wrestling, and the competition quickly restored the strength he had lost while he was ill.

Straight Arrow had come full circle with his father, and now it was he who showed He-Who-Goes-First some tricks to increase his accuracy with the bow. They trained with both the short bow and also the heavy, long-distance archery that Straight Arrow was especially skilled at. He-Who-Goes-First nodded as his son's coaching visibly increased his accuracy. In return, He-Who-Goes-First trained with his son and showed him the advanced moves of an expert swordsman. They also spent hours throwing their battleaxes. This game had evolved into a friendly competition between father and son. By winter's end, each had become a master at hitting a target with this weapon, which now made it more than just a close combat tool.

Much too soon for Gerka, she found herself once again standing in the door of her ger, holding her daughter's hand as she watched her husband and son ride off with the other soldiers. She had never gotten used to it, though she had done this so many times before. The dog stood nearby, wanting to follow the men, though not willing to leave the little girl. She was comforted by her furry friend as she watched her father and brother leave. She did not yet fully understand what they had to leave for, though she sensed the worry and sadness it brought to her mother.

Chapter 12:
Back in the Saddle

They had not traveled far when the order came to set up camp. The men occupied themselves with their duties, and soon the camp was bustling with activity. Soon after, the call came for them to assemble. As they awaited the next orders, a group of men rode into the camp. In the middle was a man dressed in great finery who was riding a splendid black stallion that was larger than the horses that his guards were riding. The man was surrounded on all sides by the well-armed men. The soldiers all watched from the assembled ranks as the visitors entered the camp and stopped.

He-Who-Goes-First was near the front of the assembly, standing with his son Straight Arrow. They stood silently and watched as the men dismounted and were greeted by the generals. It was then that He-Who-Goes-First recognized the man who stood before the army. It was Jenghiz Khan himself!

The Khan addressed the soldiers as his brothers. He praised their military conquests and boasted of the empire that they had helped to create. It was exhilarating to hear his speech, though, due to the large number of men present, not all were afforded a view such as He-Who-Goes-First and his son now enjoyed.

After his speech, the Khan waved his arm at the mass of men and ordered that they prepare food and organize contests. This was to be a joyful day with his men! The warriors relaxed, though all were visibly in awe of the unexpected visitor. He-Who-Goes-First recounted to Straight Arrow the story of his one other meeting with Temuchin. The young man listened to the story with great interest, though he had heard this tale before. Now the story had taken on life in the form of a real man who was currently in their presence.

During a contest of archery, Straight Arrow demonstrated his skill, which surpassed that of any of the personal bodyguards of the Khan. The men who lost the competition to the young man showed no emotion, though it was likely that they were less than pleased that this man, who was nearly a boy, had defeated them so soundly.

He-Who-Goes-First participated in the wrestling competition and did very well. There was one man who was one of the Khan's personal guards who spoke very little. He was nearly as wide as he was tall, though he was built solid so that even the muscles of his neck stuck out in a way that made him appear very formidable. He was the Khan's champion, and He-Who-Goes-First was asked to wrestle this man.

It was a good match, but ultimately, He-Who-Goes-First was defeated. The champion held out his hand and helped He-Who-Goes-First to his feet. He bowed to the smaller warrior and indicated that this man was a very worthy opponent. Though he was now tired from his struggle, the reputation of He-Who-Goes-First prompted another demonstration—this time with the sword. It was a non-lethal contest against the Khan's best swordsman.

Again, the match was exciting, as the skill of the two participants was at a level that few had ever witnessed before. In the end after several minutes of dueling, the Khan's guard lay on his back as He-Who-Goes-First swung and stopped his blade inches from the other man's heart. The men roared in appreciation, and He-Who-Goes-First reached down and helped the other man to his feet. He bowed to the other swordsman, and then He-Who-Goes-First returned to his ten, who were now collecting on the wagers that they had won as a result of his victory.

The Khan was pleased with the contests he saw, and he announced that he would participate in a horse race to be held next. He-Who-Goes-First had the fastest horse in the army, and while he was skeptical about the wisdom of riding against the Khan, he was persuaded by his comrades to join the competition. The course was set, and a hundred men were mounted on the best horses in all the land. The Khan sat on his black stallion as it tossed its head and snorted in anticipation. He-Who-Goes-First was atop of the gray mare, and she was equally excited to begin the race.

The wind was slight, and the sunshine had made for a very pleasant day. Above the racers, an eagle graced the event with its presence. It seemed that the entire world was eager for the race to begin. The general gave the signal, and the horses charged across the expanse.

He-Who-Goes-First found himself hemmed in between a group of riders at the start, and the Khan had pulled easily to the front of the race. As the animals began to space themselves, the gray mare took off in pursuit of the black stallion. She stretched her body in precision movements that soon brought her neck-to-neck with the larger horse. The other racers were now far behind as the finish line loomed just ahead.

As the great stallion sped forward, both he and his rider noticed the gray form move up on their left and shoot forward. He-Who-Goes-First and his mare passed over the finish line a full two body lengths ahead of the Khan's stallion. The men all cheered at the wondrous performance. Never before had they seen a race with two such splendid animals.

He-Who-Goes-First cantered his mare back to the finish line after running past and slowing his horse down. She breathed hard as they stopped. The Khan rode up next to them and got off of his stallion, which was puffing great steaming breaths into the air. Jenghiz approached He-Who-Goes-First and held out his hand in congratulations. The two men stood together as a cheer rolled through the excited audience.

The Khan wasted no time in asking if he could buy the gray mare from He-Who-Goes-First. Seconds went by as those who were present could feel the tension of the moment. Then the leader of ten spoke his answer to the leader of all.

"I cannot part with this animal willingly," he began. "She is more than just a horse to me. She is a friend, a protector and a loyal member of my family. Together, we have served the Khan well, and together we have defeated many enemies on the battlefield. Without her, I am He-Who-Goes-First; but with her, I am invincible!"

The Khan stood motionless, absorbing the words of his subordinate, as if he were drinking the meaning from them. Then, slowly, he cracked a smile and spoke loudly so all could hear.

"Were you just any man, I would most likely take the animal as my own. However, you are—as are all the men of my great army—my brother! You shall have your great horse, and any man who tries to take it from you will have to answer to Jenghiz Khan!"

The men watching all looked in disbelief as the Khan patted the gray mare and then took the reigns of his magnificent black stallion and led it away. Slowly, the group erupted into a cheer. The Khan believed in a code of honor, and he recognized it in the loyal warrior who had won this contest fairly. To do anything less than congratulate him would have dishonored the Khan in the eyes of his men. What they had witnessed here proved to them that Jenghiz Khan was a fair ruler who valued the men who were in his army. He had decreed before them all that no man, including the Khan himself, would take the prized mare from the man known as He-Who-Goes-First.

* * * *

As the Khan's army continued into foreign territory, they became more adept at the siege tactics that had served them so well in China. Jenghiz Khan had acquired the equipment for laying siege, which he used to build on his army's superiority on the battlefield, to propel it into an ability to conquer fortified cities. Some of this history predated the active participation of He-Who-Goes-First. He had heard tales of how the use of battering rams, catapults and explosives had destroyed the walls that had previously held them at bay.

Some of these battles had to be fought again, as the Khan did not always have the luxury of occupying a defeated region. After his conquests in China, he had continued on into the Islamic controlled areas farther to the west. He-Who-Goes-First had joined the Khan's campaigns during this later period. In the early days of the empire,

Chapter 13:
The Enemy Within

The Khan's army was heading home, but they were taking the long way back. Continual uprisings occurred in the far reaches of the empire, and it was only wise to visit these localities on the return trip. Most of the problems were minor…once the Mongol army arrived. After they moved on, however, the situation was sometimes very different.

He-Who-Goes-First was quieter than usual. He was still brooding about his friend's death. He wanted to get home to Gerka and their daughter. He was feeling uneasy. He had a strong desire to go home right at that moment, and these side trips were weighing heavily on his patience. Straight Arrow tried to help by distracting his father, but he was only successful for brief moments at a time.

* * * *

Inside of her ger, Gerka lay silently. She had lost a lot of blood. Her daughter was sleeping nearby. The miscarriage had come in the night, and Gerka had made no sound. Her situation was serious, but she would survive the night. She tried to cover the fetus and the blood as best as she could. She did not want her daughter to wake up frightened by the blood. She was angry with her husband. It was not a calculated or even a logical reaction; it just was. He-Who-Goes-First had missed the birth of their daughter, and he was unable to help her now.

She felt the wetness of her own blood beneath her. She wanted to be held and comforted, but her man was away…again…with the army in some foreign land. She would bear her burden silently…alone…again. A single tear slowly moved down her cheek as she thought about the lifeless form that had come from within her. She could not bear to look at him again. When the light came…when she could stand again, she would bury it.

The next day, if she could not rise, she would send her daughter to bring Straight Arrow's wife. She would help. For the time being, she could only lay silently in the dark and wonder if her husband was thinking about her, or if he would ever return home. The nights were very long without him. Slowly, she drifted off to sleep.

* * * *

He-Who-Goes-First was sleeping under the sky, wrapped in a blanket. At dawn, he awoke to the sound of someone walking nearby. He opened his eyes in time to see Soonok walk past. The sight made him uneasy. This man was an enemy who lived within the ranks of the same army. He-Who-Goes-First decided to rise himself.

He relieved himself and started back for his camp when Soonok appeared again.

"Why are you here?" demanded He-Who-Goes-First.

"I am a soldier in the Khan's army," Soonok replied smugly.

"Why do I wake to the sound of you near and find you stalking me now?" asked He-Who-Goes-First.

"Perhaps you had better return to your camp; you might get hurt out here," snarled Soonok.

Wasting no more words, He-Who-Goes-First lunged at Soonok, who swung at He-Who-Goes-First with a dagger. He-Who-Goes-First caught the wrist that held the knife, and he hit his enemy in the throat with his other fist. Soonok gasped for air as He-Who-Goes-First removed the knife from his hand and tossed it away.

Others in the camp were awakened by the scuffle, and soon they formed a ring around the two combatants. As far as He-Who-Goes-First was concerned, he had unarmed his nemesis and the fight was over. Soonok was not ready to give up though, and he charged with his fists ready. He-Who-Goes-First had reached his breaking point. The stress of the past few weeks welled up inside of him, and he proceeded to put an end to the harassment he was enduring from Soonok.

He-Who-Goes-First was beyond being concerned about injury. He was beyond worrying about injuring Soonok. He was undaunted by any possibility of punishment from the generals for his action. Plain and simple, he was fed up!

Straight Arrow reached the circle in time to see his father reach his full fury. He-Who-Goes-First used his clenched fists to pummel the face of his tormenter. Soonok tried to fight, but he was overwhelmed by the quickness and ferocity that he had unleashed upon himself. It took only seconds for Soonok to fall, and He-Who-Goes-First jumped on top of him and continued the assault. Others came to the rescue, and it took four men to pull He-Who-Goes-First off.

One of the generals asked if there was any transgression that he needed to address.

"No," replied He-Who-Goes-First. "I think this man has learned his lesson."

"And you?" questioned the general of Soonok.

"No," replied Soonok through a bleeding mouth.

Many of the soldiers remembered the fight between these two men that had culminated in the sky breathing fire down upon them. No one was anxious to repeat such an event. The general was satisfied to overlook the fight...if it was over. It was not entirely uncommon for a skirmish to erupt amongst a group of warriors. If it was to continue, however, something might need to be done. Sometimes the men just needed to take care of these aggressions themselves.

He-Who-Goes-First was an honorable man, and he was not known for fighting—except on the battlefield. Soonok had been problematic at times. He was not a particularly cooperative man, and he had not made any real impact, either good or bad, on the army as a whole. He was typically a loner, and he neither stood out as an asset or a liability. He did seem to have a problem with He-Who-Goes-First, however. At the present time, though, the general had more important things to worry about.

The army mounted up and prepared to cross the desert. The sun was hot, and the trip would be hard. He-Who-Goes-First had learned that there were many inhospitable places in the world. This he knew from experience. The journey was largely uneventful. The only means of survival was sometimes the blood they drank from their horses. When they finally found water, they had to take precautions so that their thirsty animals did not drink too much at one time. The water was often watched by bandits who made their living by preying on travelers. This was not a problem for the Khan's army. Large armies had perished before them, and for a small group to attack such a force was suicide.

They visited a number of cities on the journey home. Most stops were short, and the inhabitants gave the supplies and tribute requested. It was more cost-effective than risking a military assault. There was one kingdom that did refuse to allow the Khan's envoy in. The banner waved, and the siege weapons were brought forward on two-wheel carts. The bombardment lasted long enough for the Mongol generals to lose their patience. The city was sacked and burned to the ground.

He-Who-Goes-First did his duty to his Khan, but his heart was back home with his wife. Something was making him feel uneasy, and he wanted to cease these meandering side trips and head back home. Gerka needed him; he was sure of it. He did not know why, but he wanted to return to the land of his birth, and he did not want to wait any longer.

* * * *

When He-Who-Goes-First finally made it to his wife's ger, she gave him a rather unenthusiastic welcome. He did not understand why she was so cold, but he attempted to settle back into domestic life. Gerka performed her duties as his wife without emotion. She was distant, and it hurt He-Who-Goes-First within his heart. He had been relieved to find his family safe and healthy. He was unaware of the miscarriage or the reason for his wife's change in mood.

That night, he held Gerka close, but he felt that she was still very far away. He asked her what was troubling her, but she stubbornly refused to share what was going on inside of her. She held tightly to the pain that she felt, and the resentment was growing inside of her. Now that her husband was home, she could have reached out to him for comfort, but her pride prevented her from sharing her feelings with him.

After his frustrations of the past few months away from his beloved wife, He-Who-Goes-First was at a loss to understand why she now chose to shut him out. He found momentary solace in his interactions with his daughter. The little girl was still growing quickly, and he felt a sense of sorrow over the time he had lost with her while he traveled the Khan's empire. He wondered if he could take leave from the army for a while. When his interactions with Gerka did not improve, he wondered if he wanted to stay home at all.

He pondered the fact that he had tried so hard to deal with his emotions and his sense of loss when he was away. The feelings had been complicated by the death of his childhood friend. All he had wanted to do for the last few weeks was to come home. Now, when he was with his wife and daughter, his wife remained distance and silent. His world was broken. Depression sapped his energy, and he was not interested in hunting, riding or contests. Straight Arrow was worried about his father, but he was unable to get to the source of the problem. He did sense a change in Gerka, and he was sure that something was wrong. Had she fallen in love with another man? Straight Arrow asked his own wife this question, but she said that Gerka had no other man.

He-Who-Goes-First was not sure what to do about the situation. He tried to be supportive, but Gerka would not accept his attention. He brought her presents, and she was unresponsive. He told her that he loved her, and she offered him only silence. He knew that women could be difficult to understand, but he was sure that something was wrong. He was also sure that his wife was upset about something and that the "something" was him. No matter how hard he tried, he could not please her. Finally, when the day came for him to return to the army, he embraced his daughter and left.

Back with the army, He-Who-Goes-First was sullen and moody. He was once again, battling a war within his own mind…and in his heart. He lost much sleep along the way, and he soon began to realize that this "enemy" within himself was a liability to his own survival. If Gerka would not love him, he would have to find a new reason to go on with life. He still had his daughter and his son Straight Arrow. He was also a valued member of the Khan's army.

In the first battle since his return, He-Who-Goes-First felt fatigue. He had not slept or trained like he should have. The gray mare was holding her own and even compensating for his lack of alertness and stamina. He fought as well as he could and emerged from the battle feeling like an old man. His self-doubt was weighing him down. When he finally succumbed to exhaustion, he dreamed about Gerka. He still loved her, and he still hurt deeply inside.

As the days went on, he used his mental discipline to block out the pain of his broken heart. He turned within, and banished the demons that were attacking his emotional well-being. He became darker and more somber. When he felt the pain in his heart, he trained even harder. When he felt depression, he forced himself to excel at the tasks at hand.

On the battlefield, he became dominant in all that he did. There was no fear of death inside of him. In fact, he welcomed it. Death would put an end to the pain that he kept hidden deep within the recesses of his being. But he could not meet death willingly. He was a fighter. He pursued death, and he conquered it even as he conquered those who challenged him in battle. He fought with a fury and an energy that exists within one who is possessed by a desire to forget the pain of his life. He had become as adept at wreaking death upon the Khan's enemies as he was at retiring the demons who challenged him from within. He had reached a new level as a warrior.

There is no man as dangerous as the man who believes that he has lost everything. At this moment in time, He-Who-Goes-First was

Temuchin had a more active role in the warfare; later, it was less frequent that he would appear on the battlefield.

Within the band of dedicated soldiers who fought for the Mongolian ruler, there were a small number of women warriors. They had chosen to pursue warfare, and their abilities, combined with the fact that women in this culture were influential, allowed them to be accepted into the ranks. Jenghiz Khan was an "equal opportunity" leader. He showed great interest in the knowledge and ways of those he traded with and conquered. He was also very tolerant of the religious beliefs of others. These attributes contributed to his success as a leader and a ruler.

His interest in technology afforded him the edge he had needed in many of his successes. For centuries, China had been able to repel the attacks by the "barbarians" from the north. The use of weapons of siege was effective in bringing down the walls that had previously protected the Chinese from attack. The technology for such sieges came largely from the Chinese themselves. The history between the two cultures was filled with intermittent trade and disputes.

Other innovations included armor that was lighter in weight. Metal was still used, but leather treated with a lacquer made from fish was much lighter in weight. Later, the Teutonic Knights were soundly defeated by the Mongols in spite of their bulky armor that covered them from head to toe. The large horses they rode on were shot out from under the knights, who found themselves helpless on the ground, impaired by the weight of their own protection.

Jenghiz did not like to be limited by any particular way of doing things, and he was always on the lookout for a better strategy in both organization and equipment. The men who had given their allegiance to the Khan found themselves in the most effective military force that had ever been assembled. Frequently outnumbered, they continued to defy the odds and defeat strong, established military forces. As it stood, the Khan's army was equally adept at laying siege and defeating a fortified city as it was in the decimation of an opposing army on the open battlefield.

The truth of warfare is less glorious for those who lie bleeding on the field of battle and for their families and friends who are left behind. Tragedy and warfare go hand-in-hand, and it is this aspect that is sometimes forgotten after sufficient time passes. An event that transpired for He-Who-Goes-First during one battle again caused him to revisit that place inside of his mind, where the doubts about the merits of his occupation as a soldier/killer resided.

They had once again run up against a professional army, composed of hardened, slave soldiers in the far western portion of the empire. The Mongols had some success in defeating the enemy, but they had suffered many casualties in the process. In the end, nightfall had the final decision to postpone the activities of war.

As the respective forces pulled back when the darkness came, He-Who-Goes-First helped to remove the dead and injured from the battlefield. The bodies were lined up in rows as they were carried away from the field where they had fallen. This was a process that was never enjoyable, though it was one of the inevitable aspects of war. As He-Who-Goes-First finished moving his last burden, he happened to notice the body of his childhood friend. They were both proud warriors in the Khan's army, but now his friend was lying twisted on the ground near the end of one of the rows of corpses. His head was in an odd position, and He-Who-Goes-First noticed that it was because he had nearly been decapitated. His body had been trampled by men and horses before being removed from the battlefield.

He-Who-Goes-First knelt near his friend as a single tear fought through the dirt, sweat and blood that was caked on his face. They had been friends since the earliest of his memories. While they had less association as they grew older, He-Who-Goes-First found himself very distraught over the lifeless body of his old friend. He remembered the days of their youth and the fun they had while caring for the horses of their fathers. Both men had lost their fathers to war and had become soldiers themselves. They both knew the dangers involved, but this was the life that had been destined for them.

He-Who-Goes-First sat near the body of his friend as the night fought back the day. He remained for some time, silently communing with the spirit of his old friend. He regretted letting so much time pass between them without more than a few words of small-talk. They had drifted apart, as friends so often do. Life had changed for them both since the days of their youth. Now he was dead. He was yet another victim of the continuous warfare that dominated the life of the Khan's soldiers.

He was not sure how long he had sat there, but eventually He-Who-Goes-First went to find his son. Straight Arrow had also lost a friend in that battle. He was feeling remorse for the loss and also a bit of fear about his own mortality. Father and son exchanged a few words—enough to let each other know of the misfortunes that had been bestowed upon the day. Then, they sat together in silence, waiting for the night to be defeated by the rising sun.

Neither man was ready for sleep, but before long, the combination of depression and exhaustion sent them both to the dream world. The morning came too soon, and the whole of the Khan's army had to fight fatigue before they could begin to battle the enemy.

The doubts of the previous evening had been replaced inside of He-Who-Goes-First by a desire for vengeance. It was not a calculated or even a logical reaction; it just was. He picked up his weapons and mounted his gray mare. She had a wound on her flank, but it was not bad. He had failed to see it the previous night, and he was upset with himself. Thankfully, the wound had clotted, and it appeared that it would heal on its own. This enemy was a worthy adversary, and the Mongols could only hope that the slave army was as weary as they were.

The men on both sides were capable of enduring great hardship. As the call to battle came, they engaged once more, and soon the Khan's army took control by sheer determination. They decimated the opposition; but just as it looked like victory was theirs, reinforcements arrived for the other side. It was time to pull back. The newly arriving soldiers were slow to move forward. The decimation of their elite forces weighed heavily on their bravery as they saw the extent of the losses already suffered. Bodies and body parts, along with dead horses, weapons and a river of blood littered the battlefield.

The Mongol leaders called for a retreat. They found that they were having difficulty getting beyond the territories that they had already conquered that previous fall. It was time to pull back. They had easily ridden through the previously conquered lands, but these slave-soldiers were costing them greatly.

He-Who-Goes-First had gone into battle at the front of his men. He showed no emotion and worked largely by instinct. He had retreated to the safety inside of his mind. His body was fighting the battle, and he felt as if he was only a spectator as he chopped his way through the enemy soldiers. Time was stretched, and he felt as if things were moving in slow-motion. He was fighting on, intent on taking revenge against those who had cost him his friend.

A hand touched his shoulder, and he wheeled around, sword drawn back to strike, when he noticed it was his son, Straight Arrow.

"Come, father; it is over," he said.

It took a moment to register, and all at once, the sound came rushing back to his ears as the world came back into real-time. He rode off the battlefield with his son. The army moved back, and those enemies who were foolish enough to follow did not go unchallenged.

He-Who-Goes-First, Straight Arrow and others launched their arrows into the fresh troops that pursued them. It did not take long before the enemies saw the folly of pursuing the Mongols who were now leaving anyway. As the dead and wounded were beginning to outnumber the living, the reinforcements stopped short and watched the invaders retreat. Though the Mongols had decided that they had had enough, they had suffered far fewer casualties than the other army. They were, however, stretched far beyond the limits of their safely conquered territory. Life became harder this far from home, and death was more rampant in this land than even they were used to.

most alive when he was facing death head-on. He continued to ride into battle ahead of the others. He no longer felt pain in the same way that he had before. Compared to the pain that he felt inside of his heart, all other discomfort seemed trivial. He no longer worried about what was right and what seemed wrong. Those who knew him the best saw something truly terrifying in his eyes as he rode into battle and returned stained in the blood of his enemies. This continued for some time, until he emerged coldly from battle one day and found the arrow that was buried in the chest of his beloved gray mare.

With the realization that his favorite horse had received a serious wound, he suddenly felt his emotions rush back inside of him like the waters of a flood. He enlisted the help of Straight Arrow and some of the other men. They eased the mare to the ground by holding her head and pushing down. The men held her on the ground as He-Who-Goes-First opened the wound wider with his dagger. The arrow was lodged deep enough that he had to cut into her flesh to free the barbed end. When he pulled it free, Straight Arrow slapped a hot firebrand on her chest and cauterized the wound.

The mare had held on bravely, but the fire burned her flesh, and she threw the men off of her as she rose to her feet. She reared up and prepared to strike dead all who dared to come near her. Amidst the flurry of hooves, the men rolled and dodged away from the certain death from the flailing gray demon. One man stood before her with his arms held high; it was He-Who-Goes-First.

He spoke to the horse and stood his ground as she pawed the air and bellowed in pain. He continued to chant softly to her, and moments later, she stood calmly as he rubbed her neck and patted her softly. They stood together, still covered in blood. The other men watched in stunned silence. When no man or woman could bring the emotions back to the man called He-Who-Goes-First, it was a horse that brought him back to life. He stood holding her head in his hands. A tear wound its way down his face and landed on hers.

Chapter 14:
The Healing

He-Who-Goes-First was very concerned about his horse. The injury did not appear to be life-threatening, but there was always a risk that the wound could fester and death could come later. There was no understanding of the biological causes of such things, yet the potential outcome was well-known. He took extra care with his prized mare, and he chose not to ride her in battle. This made things difficult, as the mare did not like to be left behind any more than He-Who-Goes-First liked being without her.

The mare he chose to ride in the first battle was prone to fear at just the wrong times. He would have worked with the animal, but he had grown accustomed to his gray mare and her uncanny senses and bravery. The second time he rode into battle, he was on a fine stallion that he had trained with for several days. This horse performed well under the stress of battle, but as fortune would have it, the stallion was shot out from under him. The arrow had gone through the neck of the horse, and it lay on the ground coughing blood and struggling until a merciful thrust of the sword ended its agony.

He-Who-Goes-First fought on foot for most of the rest of that battle, until he found a horse that was riderless and swung onto the animal's back. He finished the battle on this horse, and it took his directions well, for a first time collaboration. After the fighting ended, He-Who-Goes-First found the warrior whose horse he had been riding. The other man had fallen off during the course of the battle, and he had been separated from his mount. It was a good Mongol pony, which He-Who-Goes-First returned to its rightful owner.

As the weeks went on, the gray mare improved quickly. The slight limp she had was rapidly disappearing. He-Who-Goes-First exercised her on a lead, and soon he was taking her for short rides around the camp. The mare had a desire to run beneath her master again. This loyalty and dedication was admirable in any animal or man. This was the drive that made this horse so special. Her will to live sped her recovery until she had once again regained her place with He-Who-Goes-First.

He-Who-Goes-First was healing too. His internal wounds were mending, and he was again thinking about his wife Gerka. Would she still be unable to love her husband, or would she also have begun to heal? He-Who-Goes-First was not sure what to expect when he returned to her. He did know that he could not stand to live with his woman under the conditions that had existed during their last time together. Perhaps she would divorce him, or maybe he would have to leave her. He hoped that they could return to the relationship that they had previously known.

The bond between He-Who-Goes-First and Straight Arrow was quickly reestablished. He-Who-Goes-First was able to break free of his depression, and he had regained his emotions when he almost lost his favorite horse. The world did not seem so bleak these days, and he had regained his sense of humor. He-Who-Goes-First, the storyteller, was once again the favorite entertainer around the campfire. Wherever he sat in the evening, there was sure to be a large group of warriors listening to his tales. The men joked and laughed the hours away.

The presence of He-Who-Goes-First was powerful. The past few weeks had been tense, as he had been quiet and moody. His aura was hard to ignore, and now that it was shining brightly again, the camp seemed to be a more cheerful place. Soonok had drifted into the fringes of the camp, and he was all but forgotten these days.

Straight Arrow enjoyed a special place at his father's fire. He was usually seated next to his father, and occasionally he played the role of the "straight man." He-Who-Goes-First was always coming up with new observations that he incorporated into his stories and jokes. He seemed to deal with daily adversity by discovering the absurdity of everyday things.

* * * *

Since her husband had left, Gerka had also been in a depression. Her resentment and anger had become sadness soon after He-Who-Goes-First departed. She wanted to tell him that she was sorry. That was no easy task for her. She was a proud woman who preferred to have things her own way. Her husband's dominant personality sometimes prompted her to challenge him unnecessarily. She knew that he let her get by with liberties that he would not accept from others. She also knew that he did have a "breaking point," and she really didn't want to cross it.

As she made food for herself and her daughter, she wished that she could let her husband know that she still loved him. If he was home now, she would put her arms around his neck, and no words would be needed. She was uneasy with the thought that he might be killed and never return to her. Their last moments together were not how she wanted to remember him. They had once shared something so wonderful, and she needed him more than she wanted to admit…even to herself.

* * * *

He-Who-Goes-First lay in his blanket. He could not sleep. Some nights he volunteered to keep watch because of his insomnia. He would eventually reach a state of exhaustion. More than once, Straight Arrow had found his father standing on night watch, struggling to stay alert. He would take up the watch and send his father to bed. A few hours later, He-Who-Goes-First would be awake again.

The man who could rule the battlefield was defenseless to protect himself from his own emotions when it came to his wife. He quickly forgot about the bad things, and he remembered how much he loved her. If only she would feel the same about him! He would think about her as he looked up at the star-filled sky...and with her name on his lips, he would finally fall asleep.

* * * *

The Mongol army was poised on the edge of a city. The sky was overcast, and there was a slight mist in the air. The messenger had entered the gates and there was no answer as of yet. The generals were becoming impatient. Then it happened. The body of the Khan's messenger tumbled down from above the wall that protected the city...then his head came down behind it. The body parts hit the ground with a sickening thud. As He-Who-Goes-First scanned the top of the wall, he could see that it was lined with archers.

The implements of siege were wheeled forward. The catapults launched stones and flaming bales of hay. A group of men worked on the gate with a battering ram, until those on the inside poured scalding hot oil over the top. The resistance was increasing the anger of the Mongol generals, and the likelihood that this city would survive was decreasing by the minute.

The barrage continued until the fortifications began to crumble. It was too late for surrender. The Mongols charged through the destruction and began their complete annihilation. He-Who-Goes-First was on foot, walking through the enemy as they fell before his sword. Within minutes, the entire place was burning. Anything that was not looted was burned. Anyone who was not carried away was killed.

As the soldiers worked their way through the broken inferno, He-Who-Goes-First noticed a young woman in a tower near the center of the city. Smoke billowed from the window she was standing in. She held a small child close to her chest, and then she dropped it to the ground. There was no surviving such a fall. He kept watching as she climbed out herself and jumped to her death. Flames were now visible in the window she had been occupying. He-Who-Goes-First turned away and continued his work.

The Khan's army collected their spoils and mounted up. They

turned their backs on the destruction and death that they had just inflicted on the once proud city. First blood had been drawn by the inhabitants, and now, all that was once behind their walls was gone. It was a scenario that had been repeated over and over as the Mongols dominated the landscape. It was this destruction that insured the Khan's supremacy. It was such consequences that caused others to surrender without a fight. It was not perpetrated with any more malevolence than what goes through the wolf's mind as he takes down his struggling prey.

He-Who-Goes-First did not tell stories around the fire that night. His absence was noticed by the others. Something was bothering him again. He had disappeared into the night, beyond the reaches of the encampment. Off…by himself…in the darkness, He-Who-Goes-First sat on the ground. His back was against a rock, and he remained motionless for several hours. In his mind he replayed the image of the woman dropping her baby from the window and then jumping herself. He thought about his wife and daughter.

Soonok had noticed He-Who-Goes-First leave the camp. He had cautiously followed his nemesis, until he suddenly felt a shiver run up his spine. The sensation was disturbing; and as he caught sight of the warrior up ahead, he thought that he could see a red-hot light emanating from the body of He-Who-Goes-First. There was an ominous feeling welling up inside of Soonok. He felt an involuntary shudder shake through his body. He remembered the beating that he had received from this enemy, and he turned and quickly headed back to camp.

A short time later, Straight Arrow walked quietly in the direction his father had gone in. In the moonlight, some distance away, he found him. He did not approach. He was satisfied that He-Who-Goes-First was nearby. Straight Arrow returned to camp and retired to his blanket. His father was a complicated man. He was unequivocally a master of warfare. Yet, he was prone to questioning the actions that he carried out.

All of the men suffered from emotional stress at times. The life of a soldier was difficult. Death was both a friend and an enemy—

just like fire. Which end of the sword you found yourself on determined whether you would live or die. Even in life, the stress and guilt incurred by distributing death throughout the lands both near and far could be overwhelming.

Out in the darkness, sitting on the ground with his back against a large stone, the warrior He-Who-Goes-First wept silently. The pain he had held inside was oozing out into the coolness of the night. His self-discipline had taken a breather, and he had only his pain to guide him now. He knew that he had done his best in all that he did, yet he could not stop the pain that swelled out of him.

He returned to his camp during the night. The sentry recognized him as he approached. They each nodded, and he slipped into his blanket without waking his son, who slept nearby.

When morning came, no words were needed. Straight Arrow knew that his father had sorted out his internal burdens. The night had afforded the opportunity to heal. The rising sun found He-Who-Goes-First ready to take on whatever life had to offer. As they made ready to break camp, the soldiers heard the sound of laughter. They smiled when they saw He-Who-Goes-First and Straight Arrow enjoying a good joke. The day was clear and bright. The healing had begun.

Chapter 15:
The Dream World

He-Who-Goes-First was finally able to sleep again. When he did, he found himself entering the dream world. This was the place where he had spent every night when he was a child. It had all seemed so real, and he dreamed in color. His mother was a wise person. She had told him that the dreams he had were not real. This helped some, but as he grew older, he was more and more convinced that his dreams and visions—both nocturnal and while awake—were more than just the rantings of his imagination.

The dark of night had sent shivers through his body when he was a child. This could be explained by the difficult times he was born into. Temuchin had not united the nomads of the steppe until the later years of his childhood. The transition had taken place during his father's lifetime. His father had gone from warring with other tribes to uniting with them under the leadership of Jenghiz Khan. That meant that the violence of war had been closer to home in those earlier days. It was scary for a child to be awakened by a raiding party attacking his village.

Yet there was more to it than that. He-Who-Goes-First had a suspicion that the ghosts and the voices of his youth may have been real. It had started when he was so young that he had no understanding beyond the terror that they brought. At times, he felt as if he were hearing the voices of everyone else, all at once. He could not make out the meaning of the words, because of the sheer quantity of voices that all spoke simultaneously.

That was the first time that he recalled having to force something out of his mind. He had closed the "door" on the noise. He had to learn how to filter out what was coming from the world he lived in and what was coming to him from beyond his world. Even at the time, he had doubts as to the reality of what he was experiencing. His mother told him that it was "only dreams." He had learned early that dreams may or may not have some significance in the "real" world. But what about the visions that came while he was awake? Was there something wrong with him? Was he "malfunctioning" somehow?

He had successfully driven the "demons" back, and he had become a successful soldier within the mighty army of Jenghiz Khan. He had conquered all the fears of his childhood. He could stand against any raiding party, whether it was day or night. The darkness had even become his friend when he was doing reconnaissance work.

He did have visions of his father. His father's spirit appeared on occasion with some advice or a riddle. His mother's death had occurred sometime after the death of his father. He was already a young man when she died in her sleep after suffering from a severe cough that would not go away. She had appeared to him only once in the dream world. It was a fleeting vision—as if she only wanted to wish her son farewell.

The feelings that occurred after such an event stuck with him for a long while after. He was prone to analyzing things, whether they were of this world or not. Despite his tendency to run headlong into battle, he was actually a cautious man. His need to engage the enemy quickly was mostly his way of combating his boyhood fears. Anything and everything that made his heart beat quickly and caused him to feel anxiety, he had taken on as his personal battle. In the end, he had reached a point in his life where he feared almost nothing—at least in the sense that others might experience fear.

He was secure in the common belief of his people that death was not the ultimate end. Reincarnation was an accepted philosophy. His experiences in the corporeal world and the dream world (or other world) had solidified this belief for him. He believed in fate, yet he knew that he had some power to influence the world he lived in. He was sure that there were powers greater than he, both in flesh and blood and in spirit. It was the spirit world that he felt most unsure of, yet he had a sense that he understood it better than most of the people he knew.

This acknowledgement of spirit and the forces of good and evil were the causes of his periodic doubts about the merits of killing and making war. Of this, however, he felt that he was powerless to influence much change. That left the question of whether he had free will to decide if he should participate in it or not. This track of thought was nearly treason for a soldier within the Khan's army. Jenghiz was considered to be a leader of great knowledge and understanding, and indeed he was. He-Who-Goes-First had an awareness, or a personal sense of morality, that expanded beyond the simple reaches of military campaigns and the subjugation of entire populations.

His understanding was partially within the other world. This concept of a spiritual realm was not foreign in the culture that he was born into. It was accepted that there were spirits inhabiting both animate and inanimate objects. It was normal for the bonds of the spirit to outweigh those of flesh or blood. This was characterized in the bond between He-Who-Goes-First and Straight Arrow. They were father and son in every way except biologically. This fact had no bearing on their lives in the way that it might affect a person from a different culture.

Now, as he had regained his ability to sleep, the dream world began to return to the forefront of his existence. He was dreaming with great clarity, and the memories and feelings were often retained when he woke up. Some of the dreams were enjoyable, and others were disturbing. He often found himself in battle with monsters of the like he had never seen on Earth. He frequently prevailed in these dreams, but he also experienced paralysis and other impediments to his movements.

He became aware of a region of his body that was often injured in his dreams. The damage occurred in that portion of his back that was nearest to his heart. Though he could feel the wound in his dreams, he was usually unable to feel any pain. The blood would flow red in vivid streams from both his back and chest. In his waking hours, he had, in times of stress, felt his heart ache within his chest. Such a pain he had felt during his last moments with his wife, Gerka.

He wondered how Gerka was. She had appeared in his dreams frequently for a while, but as time went on, she was replaced by battles and apparitions. These dreams came often, and they felt real. On one occasion, the monster that pursued He-Who-Goes-First had the voice of a man and the talons and beak of an eagle. It ran on four legs like a horse, but it was larger than four horses put together. The beast warned him to turn away and head back in the direction that he had come from. He-Who-Goes-First knew that he needed to pass the great monster, though he was not sure exactly why. He told the menacing giant that he was a member of the Khan's army, and he only needed to pass and continue his journey away from this land.

The monster clicked its curved beak and spoke its warning once again. To pass this place would mean certain death, it told He-Who-Goes-First. The warrior pulled his sword, and the battle began. The monster grasped He-Who-Goes-First in its talons as the Mongol chopped at the giant raptor's foot with his sword. The monster dropped He-Who-Goes-First, and though he was bleeding in the usual place from his back and chest, he was able to run past the demon, where he found himself falling through some expanse on the other side.

The thought occurred to He-Who-Goes-First that perhaps he should have listened to the monster. Then he began to realize that this might be a dream! Such revelations frequently resulted in He-Who-Goes-First waking up, but he was able to maintain this dream and continue on the journey to see what enlightenment he might gain from the experience.

That was when he stopped falling. He found himself resting on the helmet of a giant warrior. The soldier was unaware of the presence of He-Who-Goes-First, who was but a mere speck in the presence of such a huge man. The dreaming Mongol was assessing his situation, when he noticed that far below, the ants that ran in terror beneath the giant's feet were screaming in his native tongue. That was when he realized that they were not ants, but rather they were actually people of a very small stature!

How astounding that there might be such a difference in size between two creatures that appeared in all other ways to be human beings! Was this the way that the world was organized? One who was so small could not perceive the world of the giant, nor could the giant know that the specks he trampled were actually living people!

He-Who-Goes-First's current size within the parameters of his dream allowed him to see into both "worlds." The tiny people were unaware that the "natural catastrophe" that was befalling their city had its origins in an oversized giant who didn't know any better. This was an idea that brought He-Who-Goes-First back to "reality" with a jolt. He woke excitedly, and he lay awake for a long time contemplating the meaning of this dream.

The world of flesh and blood may be separated by the spirit world in a variety of ways. The thought had never occurred to him that size could be one of them. If the past, present and future were divisions, and so was size, there could be any number of other reasons why the world of flesh and blood existed separately from the spirit world. Perhaps the divisions were not so great that someone might not be able to possess the ability to see portions of one world, while still existing in the other…as a living, breathing person!

The idea no longer seemed like just a possibility, but rather it seemed like it was probable. Those things that had terrified He-Who-Goes-First as a child may actually be valuable. That "sense" that he had in times of danger—or the knowledge of something that came from that same place where the wolf finds his truth—could be emanating from between two existences or two "worlds." This was all fascinating to a man who had previously thought that he lived primarily to kill those who stood in the way of the Mongol Empire.

Was this knowledge that he had gained by defying the monster that blocked his passage a gift or a curse? Was the warning real? Now that He-Who-Goes-First had gained this new sense of understanding, would he be satisfied to continue on as a member of the Khan's army? It was all very exciting and a little bit disquieting. He-Who-Goes-First felt as if his head was ready to burst with the new ideas that were brought to life on this night.

These new ideas bore so much weight in his mind that he soon began to grow tired. The night was not over, and the dream world was coming through stronger than ever. He closed his eyes and drifted back to sleep.

Chapter 16:
A New Man

The recent experiences in the dream world had a significant impact on He-Who-Goes-First. He reevaluated his priorities and was eager to return to Gerka and their daughter. He was also experiencing a renewed sense of patriotism for the Mongol Empire. For centuries, his people were much maligned by the Chinese and others as simple barbarians. The ingenuity of the Khan was showing the people of the world that the nomads from the steppe were as intelligent as they were ruthless.

The pride he felt for the empire that he was helping to create provided the incentive that he needed to perform well on the battlefield. He had thought long and hard about his position in this life, and he finally decided that his course was honorable. There was also a natural order to the world, with the strong being dominant over the weak. His people had been near the bottom of that order until they were united under the rule of Jenghiz Khan. The Chinese were among the first to be made aware of the new order that had been assembled by the Mongolian leader.

He-Who-Goes-First felt no sympathy for the Chinese emperor. His time had come and gone. There was still much work to be done in that region, but the power of the Chinese had proven less than adequate to repel the forces of Jenghiz Khan. He-Who-Goes-First remembered the stories his father had told him about the glorious battles he had participated in against the Chinese.

As the Mongol Horde continued to expand into the areas of the Middle East, many more people were brought under the rule of the

Khan. There were difficulties in maintaining such a huge empire. Many of the people were rebellious, and distances proved to be an effective barrier against complete control of these outer regions. It was true that the Mongol armies were often significantly outnumbered by the armies that they defeated. Also true was the fact that occupying all the lands within their influence was simply not possible. Despite this major difficulty, Jenghiz Khan had taken control of an empire that stretched farther than anyone could have ever previously imagined.

He-Who-Goes-First had come to terms with his spirituality in battle—the same way he did when he was hunting. He killed, and then he honored the spirits of the dead later. He was following the natural laws of life and death. He could feel the power vibrating through his body when he went to war. His body was compact and solid. His arms and legs were muscular, and his chest was large. His back was wide, and he possessed great strength. He enjoyed the feel of his sword, and he could be seen training with it often. He could swing the sword furiously from side to side and around and around. Such calisthenics could be dangerous for just anyone, but to He-Who-Goes-First, his sword was almost an extension of his own body.

By this time, his body was decorated by a variety of scars. The numerous battles he had engaged in had not left him unscathed. Most of these injuries were not severe, and more than once he had entered a military campaign with some significant pain or an existing wound. This was all part of the difficulties that were surmounted daily within the ranks of the Khan's army. There was no sympathy for someone who could not withstand hardship. It was expected and even necessary. Those who were unable to deal with the stress and pain of a soldier's life were culled from the force via natural selection. They did not seem to last long in battle.

The hard life of the people of the steppe had produced a hardy breed of warrior. Centuries of warfare and raids had ensured that only the strongest survived long enough to reproduce. There were no weaklings among the Khan's men. The strength and courage of these warriors had proven to be more than a match for those who stood against them. Despite often having inferior numbers, the Mongols possessed superior strength, organization and skill.

In his mind, He-Who-Goes-First sorted through all of the knowledge and observations he had made. As he did so, he swung his sword around his head and shoulders. The silver blade was a blur as it cut through the air with astonishing speed and precision. Never did he seem to make a mistake. Even though his mind was deep in thought, his body moved perfectly on pure instinct. For all his ability to analyze his world, He-Who-Goes-First did not care to over-think his movements or actions in the arts of war or horsemanship. He was so in tune with his abilities that he could have likely done these things blindfolded. There were times, in fact, when the field of battle became so chaotic that he did fight blindly on instinct alone.

His reactions were deadly quick, and his movements showed no weakness. Along with his brothers, he inspired terror in those who met him in battle. There was no need to continue agonizing over the actions that he carried out or the dead that fell beneath his horse's feet. The battles had always been; only now his people were propelled in a unified direction under the leadership of the Khan. There had always been those who breathed victory and those who bled death. There would always be such things in the "yet to come." He was sure of it, just as he was sure of his place at the front of the charging army.

His shield and armor had been hit by arrows, and the armor of his horse had also been hit. Still, He-Who-Goes-First and the gray mare continued to be first into battle and among the last to ride out. They had been covered in the blood of hundreds and thousands of others, and still they were able to survive in spite of the death that surrounded them.

As a whole, the Khan's army was much better at inflicting casualties than it was at receiving them. It was not uncommon for a skirmish to yield devastating losses to the opposition and hardly any casualties for the Mongols. Warfare had been a way of life for the nomads of the steppe for so long that those who had survived were hardened into the most skillful and deadly army on Earth.

He-Who-Goes-First put down his sword and began to practice with his bows. He was shooting at a target he had set up, and he was quite pleased with himself for the "bull's-eyes" he had just made. Just before he rose to retrieve his arrows, he heard a hissing sound over his right shoulder. It was followed by a dull thud. He looked back and saw Straight Arrow smiling several paces behind him. The single arrow that he had shot landed between the grouping of bull's-eyes in the middle of his father's target.

He-Who-Goes-First nodded in appreciation of his son's skill. There was still no doubting that he was the best archer in the Khan's army. The young man had grown tall and lean, and his physical power was evident in the lean muscles of his body. He had seen much military action in his young life, and he had continued to excel in the art of warfare. He was gaining notoriety among the generals for his unique ability to assess a battlefield. He had become something of a tactician, and his input was never disregarded. If not for his youth, he would likely have gained much influence in the army, but there was still time for that.

Chapter 17: The North

As the Khan's army headed toward the north, the steppe gave way to taiga. They came to Lake Baykal and set up their camp. The air was crisp, though it was now summer. The lake was large, and He-Who-Goes-First enjoyed being near the water. He had in his travels seen the Caspian Sea to the west and had visited the Yellow Sea in Manchuria to the east. He liked being near to the water very much. He had also been in the mountains many times, and he enjoyed the elevations as well. His travels with the Khan's army had given him the opportunity to see many wondrous things.

The nomads were said to have come from this region to the north. Indeed, as they traveled farther into the northern forests, they saw signs of wolves, who were the ancestors of the people. There was much game here, and the men were eager to hunt. The size of their force was not conducive to stealth, so the men needed to go out in smaller groups in search of game.

The people they met were eager to trade, and there was no reason to conquer their villages. There was no treasure there, except for the timber and furs that were abundant in this land. Each evening when they made camp, the men were able to hunt for deer and other wild beasts that lived in the forest. He-Who-Goes-First was eager to go hunting with his son, Straight Arrow. The two set out with four horses in search of game.

They traveled into the thick forest and decided to wait in ambush in an area that seemed to be filled with the signs of life. There was a small clearing and plenty of cover to hide in nearby. There were tracks and droppings, and it would only be a matter of time before something showed up. They left their horses close by and faced into the wind, waiting for unsuspecting prey to wander near. The sun was shining, but the timber was dense, and it shaded the cool ground.

The first to wander past was a small group of three wolves. They circled through the area, noses to the ground in search of the fresh scent of game. They stopped and tested the wind with noses and ears. Something wasn't right, and they may have sensed the presence of the two men who were hiding close by. Straight Arrow was motioning that they should shoot, but He-Who-Goes-First would not have any part in the killing of their ancestors. The wolves were simply of a different tribe, he later told his son, and under the Khan, the tribes were now united.

They continued to wait until they were rewarded with the appearance of a small group of deer. It was hard to tell exactly how many there were, due to the thick growth. The deer set out to eat some of the brush that was growing so densely at the edge of the clearing, and the two warriors armed their bows as they maintained their silence. With a quick glance to ensure that they both were ready, the hunters shot simultaneously, and the brush exploded as the animals scattered. The powerful bows they used had propelled their arrows with great force, and each man had hit a deer.

They sprung from their hiding place and ran toward their quarry. The deer that He-Who-Goes-First had hit was a large buck. It had dropped to the ground, but its head was still up, and it was struggling to stand. He-Who-Goes-First fired a second arrow into the animal's throat, and it stopped struggling. A slice from his sword ensured the end. Straight Arrow's deer had bolted after it was hit, and the trail showed that it was bleeding profusely. The two men got their horses and began to follow the trail.

The wounded deer seemed intent on leading them through the most difficult terrain possible. The growth contained thorns and numerous obstacles. In the end, they had to leave their horses and continue the last of the way on foot. The doe was dead when they found her. Her brown eyes were open as she stared lifelessly at the two men who now dragged her out of the thicket. They loaded her onto one of the pack horses, and then started back to the area where the buck was lying.

When they reached the small clearing, they were surprised to find that they were not alone. A brown bear had taken control of the slain buck, and he had claimed it as his own. The two Mongols looked at each other in shock as the huge animal ripped large chunks of meat from the carcass and devoured them whole. The bear's snout was red with thick blood, and as soon as it noticed the men who were invading its mealtime, it growled ferociously and made a mock charge.

That was all it took for He-Who-Goes-First and Straight Arrow to decide to leave. There was enough meat for them on the doe, and the bear was large and angry. They might be able to kill it, but it was a risky venture. The men recognized the power of the bear, and they respected his ability to take what he wanted. It was the natural order of things for the strongest to claim his prize if it was not guarded…or if he could get away with it. Rather than being upset with the large marauder, the men saw the bear as a fellow warrior. There was no compelling reason for them to risk fighting with the beast.

As they led their horses away, the bear returned to the business of chewing and swallowing. The two men mounted their horses and turned in the direction of the camp and the other soldiers. As they rode out of the dense forest, they laughed and marveled at the things they had seen on this hunt. This forest was truly wild, and it was filled with those who hunted and those who were eaten. As they reached their camp, other men were also returning with fresh meat and stories to tell.

That night around the campfire, He-Who-Goes-First told the story of the great bear who had taken his deer. There was much laughter as He-Who-Goes-First made it clear that he was "not one to fight an unarmed bear!" Some of the men were anxious to hunt the giant brown bears that lived in this land. One of the generals gave the order that the men were to be careful with meat scraps and leftover food. He told his men that the bears were "as fearless as the Khan's soldiers, and much bigger!" Such food remnants were likely to attract unwanted visitors in the night. He also suggested that the horses be watched closely.

The next morning found the army pressing onward to the north. Most of the population of Rus was far to the west of their current position. This land was large and wild. The only real resistance that the Mongols found in this region came from the land and the weather. The farther to the north they went, the more severe the conditions became. Even the hearty warriors from Mongolia were impressed by the rugged wilderness they had entered.

Whenever the army stopped to camp, the men would go out on hunting excursions. The abundance and variety of game was such as they had never seen before. He-Who-Goes-First enjoyed spending his free time alone in the wilderness. He had learned how to be stealthy, and he enjoyed watching the animals of this domain. The wolves were a pleasure to watch. Their organization was built on the natural laws of dominance. He was able to distinguish the leaders of the pack, and he marveled at how they worked together while hunting. He saw many similarities between these animals and his own people.

He-Who-Goes-First also watched the other animals of this wilderness. He was happier to watch them than he was in hunting them. He did take meat from this land, but he still preferred to watch the bears rather than to attack them. Others from the Mongol camp could not resist the challenge of hunting the large brown bears. Groups of men were able to take these animals by surrounding one, and all those present would fire their arrows repeatedly until the beast finally fell.

The bears were incredibly resilient though. Two of the warriors were found in the forest. They had apparently challenged a large bear in combat. The animal had not given its spirit to the wind easily. Though wounded, it charged the hunters and left them torn in pieces. Other hunters tracked the great bear, and they were able to finish it off. The two unfortunate instigators were brought back to camp before their remains were buried. The skin of one had been pulled off so that it hung down over the man's face. His skull and entrails were visible. The other man was missing an arm, and he was equally disfigured.

He-Who-Goes-First preferred to watch the bears whenever he had the opportunity. From a safe place, he marveled at their incredible strength and ingenuity. He spent an evening watching a bear force a giant, fallen log over. It then proceeded to tear through the rotting wood and exposed a buffet of insects, small rodents and other bear delicacies. It was obvious to He-Who-Goes-First that these animals were not dumb, and they were much better suited to life in these harsh conditions than any man was.

Eventually the army turned toward the west, in the direction of the territories where they had waged war in the past. The farther they traveled, the more populated it became. Still, this was a large land, and it was underdeveloped compared to the areas of the Middle East or China.

While exploring the landscape by himself late one afternoon, He-Who-Goes-First was enjoying a walk in the forest. As he traveled along a stream, he heard the repeated calls of a hawk. He backtracked and scanned the treeline in the hope of locating the source of the shrill call. After a few minutes, he was able to recognize the shape of the bird in a tree on the opposite side of the stream. He stared across at the hawk and said a greeting to it, as it stared back at him. After a short time, the bird flew off in the direction that He-Who-Goes-First had been traveling in.

The warrior continued on and soon noticed that the hawk was directly above him in a tree. It was so close that He-Who-Goes-First could have thrown a rock and hit it if he had wanted to. Instead, he called out to the hawk and asked if it had a message for him. It was unusual for a man to get so close to a hawk and not cause it to fly away. He spoke calmly to the bird while it turned its head and looked down at him. It sat in the tree and listened to the man talk. Eventually, the bird took to the air again and continued upstream in the same direction as before.

He-Who-Goes-First continued on. He was heading back in the direction of his camp upstream. Before long, he noticed the hawk for a third time. It was across the stream again, sitting in the top of a tree. Once again, He-Who-Goes-First walked to the edge of the stream and spoke to the bird. He felt that perhaps there was some reason that he had thrice found it sitting in the direction of his journey. But again, despite his asking what message the hawk had for him, the bird did not speak.

He-Who-Goes-First was happy to have been honored by the hawk's presence, and he bid the bird farewell. He told it that perhaps they would meet again. The whole experience was pleasant for the warrior. He had enjoyed this excursion into the wilderness; but as the sun was getting low in the sky, he continued back to camp.

When he returned, he told his son about the hawk that had visited him. Straight Arrow agreed that this was unusual. They could not come up with any particular reason why the hawk had acted this way. He-Who-Goes-First decided that if there was a reason, it would be known in time. For the rest of the evening, he sat with his son and the other men around the fire eating the fresh meat that the wilderness had provided for them. He-Who-Goes-First told the men about his visit with the hawk, and they debated about possible reasons why such a thing might happen.

As the army continued to move toward the west, they were eventually met and challenged by a large group of armed horsemen. These were the men who lived in this harsh land, and they were not pleased by the invasion of the Khan's army. The leader spoke through an interpreter and told the Mongols to leave immediately. The warriors of Jenghiz Khan had not been challenged for quite some time, and they were eager to do battle. It did not take long before they got their wish.

The fighting was intense, and the battle was not taken to an open area as was normally the case. These warriors were more at home in the cover of the forest. Things got rather confusing once the fighting intensified. It was hard to maneuver horses and weapons in the trees. The enemy was quite adept at charging in and out of the rough terrain. It did not take long, however, for the Mongols to get the hang of this type of fighting. They had traveled through some of the densest forests imaginable to arrive at this place, and their skills in battle were already well established.

The usual complete annihilation of the opposition was not possible under these conditions, however. The survivors retreated into the wilderness and disappeared from sight. The Khan's army moved to a clearing and made their camp. In the dead of night, they were woken by the sentries, just as the foreign horsemen galloped through the camp. The attack did not last long, but the Mongols did take a number of casualties. In the end, the enemy had also lost a couple of warriors, and there were many fires to put out around the camp.

A few of the horses were missing after the attack, and morning found the Mongols in pursuit of the raiders. When the army finally arrived at the camp of those who had attacked them, the enemy was already gone, and the camp had been burned to the ground. These men were intent on staying ahead of the Khan's soldiers and destroying anything that might be useful to them.

There was no sign of the enemy until after dark. The Mongol camp was on a heightened sense of alert after the previous night's attack. This time, when the horsemen charged through the Mongol camp, they were cut down by a barrage of arrows. Their horses were shot out from under them, and the grounded enemies were chopped to pieces by the swords of the angry Mongol warriors. Those who escaped were few, and even after the attacks finally ceased, the Khan's army remained on the alert.

Chapter 18:
Searching for Answers

They continued traveling to the southwest, until after a long journey they eventually came to the northern edge of India. From here, they continued on to the west. The people that they met along the way were nomads and herdsmen, not unlike the Mongols. There was much infighting among them, like the Mongols had prior to the rule of Jenghiz Khan. While some of these men were battle-hardened, they lacked both the leadership and the cohesiveness of the Mongol warriors. The skirmishes between the two groups were generally pretty lopsided. From what He-Who-Goes-First had observed, these men were better at issuing threats than they were at carrying them out.

On one occasion, He-Who-Goes-First found himself alone, and the passage back to the rest of his army was blocked. Four of the local tribesmen shouted at him in their native language. He ignored them and attempted to pass. They drew their swords, and there was no option but to fight them all at once.

He had been warned that these men were dangerous, but he soon found that they were not as tough as their reputation had indicated. As the battle continued, not only was He-Who-Goes-First able to hold his own, he managed to increase his chances of victory by sticking his sword into the chest of one of his opponents. Obviously he had penetrated the man's lung, and blood squirted from both his victim's mouth and chest. There was a momentary wheeze of air before the man's lung collapsed, and then he dropped to his knees.

With only three left, He-Who-Goes-First was able to smash the face of a second man with his shield. The impact appeared to have shattered the man's nose. He tried to continue fighting as the blood ran down his face. He must have been in tremendous pain, and he soon lost the hand he was holding his sword with, as He-Who-Goes-First chopped it off. The severed hand and sword dropped to the ground, and the man was incapacitated and fled from the scene.

With only two men left to fight, He-Who-Goes-First caught one with the tip of his sword and ripped open his throat. The man fell to the ground as a stream of blood shot out of his carotid artery. The last man standing turned and ran.

He-Who-Goes-First had been on foot when this meeting had begun, and now he collected the four camels that his attackers had left behind. He led the camels back to the camp of the Mongol army, where the other soldiers stared at his trophies as he walked them by. He decided to keep one of the camels. He had several horses with him already, but camels were sturdy animals. He gave one to Straight Arrow and traded the other two.

He-Who-Goes-First decided that he must remember not to wander off alone because of the chance that he might find himself outnumbered again. Being outnumbered was nothing new to the Khan's army though; it was quite normal. Still, being by yourself was not a good idea. This was what he told the other men when they asked about his acquisition of the four camels. He told them that he had to fight four men, and from this, he had learned not to venture away alone. One of his comrades asked why he would worry about that if he had defeated four men by himself.

"Because next time," replied He-Who-Goes-First, "there might be five!"

The others began to laugh. He-Who-Goes-First had retained his sense of humor, and for the next few days when he wasn't riding his beloved gray mare, he was frequently seen riding his camel. Sometimes he could be heard shouting mock threats at his fellow warriors, just as the tribesmen of this region liked to do. The other soldiers thought these antics were quite amusing, and the mock boasting became quite animated and farfetched at times.

The Khan's men were able to do much trading while they roamed the area around Afghanistan. The day came, however, when they were confronted by an army intent on forcing them to leave this land. The Mongols were ready to fight, and He-Who-Goes-First had joked about riding into battle on top of his camel. When the time came, however, he was all about business. He left his sense of humor behind for the duration of the fighting as he rode straight into battle on his favorite horse.

He found that the men they fought were seasoned horsemen, but in the end, they proved to be an inferior force when matched against the military skill of the Mongol army. He-Who-Goes-First went to work with his sword. He and his mare were covered in the blood of their enemies, as was a normal condition for them while waging war. The destruction continued as the Mongols destroyed the crops and irrigation systems that they found. The message was driven home, once again, that to oppose Jenghiz Khan was always a bad policy.

Instead of continuing west, they turned to the east toward China...and home. As they passed back through the northern portion of India, they did more trading with the local people. Jenghiz Khan was as interested in trade and acquiring knowledge as he was in conquering. Often he did both, depending on what seemed to be the logical course of action under the circumstances. The wise men of India were of interest to the Khan, and a small group of three mystics were recruited to accompany the army back to meet with him. They were promised riches if they did so, and refusal to accept such an invitation might be ill-advised.

During the journey, He-Who-Goes-First took it upon himself to learn what he could from these men. They practiced breathing techniques and meditation, and the warrior found that he could incorporate some of this into his own training rituals. While the beliefs of these men were similar to his own in many ways, He-Who-Goes-First was not one to subscribe fully to anyone else's doctrines. He chose to follow the ways of the people of the steppe. Like his leader the Khan, however, he realized that there was more to the world than what was known to any one man, or any one group of people.

In a society that had expanded its boarders far beyond the reaches of their ancestors within a very short time, the knowledge that entered into the Khan's domain was as diverse as the people he had conquered and traded with. The Khan was not just a "barbarian," as many would like to believe. He was a very curious and wise man. Unlike many of the other rulers of his time, he did not destroy knowledge (or scholars) simply because he didn't understand it. He was filled with the desire to learn what he did not know, and he destroyed primarily for the purpose of instilling fear and insuring his dominance.

In many of his characteristics, He-Who-Goes-First was like the Khan, though he would never have been so bold as to say so himself. Neither man had a formal education, yet they both craved knowledge and pursued both tangible science and philosophy. He-Who-Goes-First was interested in any advances in weaponry or techniques, and he spent long hours just thinking about life and death. He struggled with his purpose on Earth and what constituted honor.

Jenghiz Khan had instituted a code of conduct that he expected his soldiers to follow. He had brought organization to chaos. He sought knowledge and violently destroyed all opposition. As He-Who-Goes-First viewed it, the Khan had brought honor to his world. Before the unification of the nomadic tribes of the steppe, no one could trust anyone else. There was so much war between neighboring tribes that chaos was the only ruler. So many things had been accomplished under the rule of Jenghiz Khan, since the days when the father of He-Who-Goes-First had first told his son about this great ruler who had emerged.

His father had seen the logic in joining with this strong leader, and that logic was still valid in the life of He-Who-Goes-First. If the Khan wanted to learn from the men of wisdom who now traveled with his army, He-Who-Goes-First would also take advantage of the chance to interact with these men when he could.

The wise men were as interested in He-Who-Goes-First as he was in them. They saw in this man someone who the others in the army looked up to. He was obviously intelligent, and he had a sense of humor that was rather attractive. In the evening, the warriors congregated around the fire of He-Who-Goes-First. They listened to his stories and were often provoked into rather interesting discussions. The men seemed to have a real desire for this type of interaction, which was perhaps normal for a group of soldiers who existed otherwise on a diet of war and travel.

The mystics were intrigued by the strength exhibited by He-Who-Goes-First, not just in battle, but in character. He was able to live in a world of violence and death and return from battle drenched in the blood of those who fell to his sword. Yet after he cleaned the blood from himself and his horse, he would sit with his brothers near the fire and make jokes while he put a new edge on the sword that he had slain countless men with. What was the answer behind the unique abilities of this man? How could he be so versatile as to be a trained and vicious killer, who could "turn it off," and spend his downtime laughing and asking the questions of a philosopher?

When He-Who-Goes-First asked questions of the wise men, they were often led into deep conversations about the world of the living and the world of the spirit. This warrior...this barbarian...this uneducated man from the land north of China was instigating discussions that led the mystics into new territories. This Mongol soldier was now adding to the knowledge of the three learned men from India.

Before long, He-Who-Goes-First did not have to seek out the wise men. They gravitated toward him, eager to resume their conversations whenever the chance came along. Straight Arrow was also interested in these discussions. He started out by listening, and as he grew more confident, he became a valued member of this new "think tank."

The men from India were very interested in the dreams and observations of He-Who-Goes-First. They found bits of significance in almost all that he said. His experience with the hawk was the subject of a lengthy discussion one evening. The wise men had no immediate answer why such a thing would happen, though they were all quite sure that there was some deeper meaning.

The men who were used to listening to the stories and jokes of

He-Who-Goes-First were now listening to the philosophical discussions that were becoming more commonplace. There was a slight shift in the usual participants, as some were more inclined to participate in the serious discussions, while others preferred the more lighthearted moments. After hammering out the philosophical matters of a particular day, He-Who-Goes-First would let out a big sigh. This was usually a sign that he had reached his limit for the evening. What followed was often a speech that started out sounding like it was serious and then ended with a punch line. That was the signal that it was time to have fun.

The crowd would shift slightly, and the laughter would begin. The three Indian mystics seemed to enjoy these lighter discussions, and they were prone to fits of laughter just like everyone else. It seemed to be a learning experience for all who participated. They were all seeking answers to the questions of life, death and spirit, of things seen and unseen. And, even if the answers may not always have been found, the important thing was that they kept looking.

Chapter 19: Crossing Over

The army was crossing over the mountains in Tibet. The air was cold in the high altitude. Summer was giving up control of the weather to autumn. The men were used to traveling, and they had crossed many mountain ranges as they journeyed back and forth throughout the Khan's empire. The terrain was rough, and the army had packed all of its burdens on a variety of animals from horses to yaks. He-Who-Goes-First found that his camel was incredibly versatile, if not always completely cooperative. It became ill-tempered from time to time, but it could carry an enormous amount of weight through harsh terrain with little food or water.

Periodically, the men were forced to dismount and lead their animals through treacherous areas. These mountain passages were difficult for the men and horses, but the land throughout the Asian Continent was filled with mountainous regions. Sometimes He-Who-Goes-First felt that the scenery was worth the extra effort. It was often possible to pass through intense heat and bone-chilling cold within hours, just by crossing over one of these mountain ranges.

As they began their descent, they eventually happened upon a group of monks who had built a monastery in the side of the mountain. The soldiers stopped and talked to the men who were living there. The monks showed the Mongols where they could get fresh water, and their hospitality impressed the leaders of the army. The men from India were interested in these mountain dwellers too, and after more talk, it was decided that two of the monks would join the travelers and continue on to meet with the Khan.

Once they were back on flat ground, the army set up camp. The group of learned men was growing on this journey, and the two new men were immediately embraced by the group of philosophers, including He-Who-Goes-First and his son. That evening the discussion by the fire included the subject of astral traveling. These monks from the mountains were interested in the dream world, and they said that they had mastered a way of leaving their bodies and traveling in spirit. They did this while asleep. They believed that the spirit was attached to the body by an invisible cord, which allowed them to return when they woke up.

They said that the sudden jolt that one experiences when waking, after hanging in between that space between being awake and being asleep, is the spirit rushing back into the body quickly before the body wakes up. He-Who-Goes-First thought about this. He had felt that sensation many times. Had he been astral traveling? He asked the monks this question. They said that it was likely that he had been. With a little guidance, he was told, he would be able to direct his spirit where he wanted it to go, and he could learn to interpret his experiences.

Of course, He-Who-Goes-First thought about Gerka. He would like to visit her. He had been away for a very long time, and he missed his wife and their daughter. He was unwilling to share this thought with the group of men who were gathered, however. It was a personal thing.

The men from India encouraged He-Who-Goes-First to share his dreams and the story of the hawk with the Tibetans. They were interested in these things, and like the Indians, they were also impressed by the intelligence of this warrior. After the talk had gone on for what felt like long enough, He-Who-Goes-First sighed, and then he began to tell a humorous story. The two monks were unaccustomed to the progression of these evening discussions, and they were taking the story as fact…until the punch line when the others began laughing. The two newcomers looked at each other, and soon they too began to smile. This experience appeared as if it might be more enjoyable than they had at first anticipated.

That night while he slept, He-Who-Goes-First's thoughts were with his wife who was still far away in the steppe. He could picture her in his mind, in the dark, inside of her ger, with their daughter sleeping next to her. He could see her face…hear her breathing…. He was transfixed on the image in his mind. All at once, he felt his body lurch, and he was awake.

* * * *

Far away, Gerka lay awake, thinking of her husband. It had been many cycles of the moon since she had last seen him. The days were growing shorter and cooler. She missed him. Why had she treated him so coldly the last time he was home? Would he ever come back to her? She lay in the dark, listening to the steady sound of her daughter's breathing. She closed her eyes as a single tear rolled down her cheek.

As she lay between slumber and wakefulness, she saw her husband's face in her mind. He looked worn from the rigors of battle and constant travel. She focused on the image of his face, and soon she could smell the scent of his body. She loved that smell and breathed in deeply. That was when she woke up startled! It took her a moment to realize where she was. Her man was not at home. She could not have smelled his body, though she was somehow sure that she had.

She wished he would come home. She would never be able to tell him how sorry she was. She was not good at sharing her feelings. Somehow she would let him know that everything was as it should be. She still loved him. She lay in the dark missing him tremendously. It would be different this time…if he would just come back to her.

* * * *

He-Who-Goes-First lay awake, thinking about what the monks had said. He had the strange feeling that what they had told him was true. He even suspected that he had done this astral traveling just now. He had seen Gerka so vividly. Even in the darkness, he saw the colors of her lips and her hair, as if she were illuminated somehow.

He felt the sweat running down his head. It was warm and wet, and as soon as the wetness touched the chill air, it took on the feeling of ice. He was trembling. It was an odd sensation for a man who was not used to the feelings associated with fear. He could hear his heartbeat…steadily beating inside of his chest. It was rapid at first, and then it slowly returned to the rhythmic drumbeat of life. He listened as the drumbeat took over his thoughts. It combined with the exhaustion he felt from his travels…and the calisthenics that he had put his mind through with the learned men…. It slowly took hold of him. His eyes drifted shut, and he fell asleep.

* * * *

The army turned toward the north and continued their journey. They were making good progress, and the men were eager to return to their families after such a long campaign. The journey led them into China, from the opposite direction that they normally entered it. The Chinese were not pleased to find out that the nomads had come up from the south. The emperor decided that he would send an army to cut them off from their homeland and any reinforcements. If they had journeyed far, they may be tired, weakened and depleted in numbers.

The Chinese would meet the Mongols in a battlefield of their choosing. It lay in the path of the invading horde, and the Chinese took time to fortify the position by sending a preliminary force to slow the Mongols down. The initial confrontation was unsuccessful, though it did buy the Chinese some extra time. These were ancient enemies who had been through many battles. The Chinese stretched their line as far as they dared, hoping to both prevent the advancing Mongols from breaking through or surrounding the Chinese fighters as they had done so many times before.

It was a good plan, except that it did not take into consideration that the force of men who came up from the south were intent on making their way to their homeland in the north, regardless of what the Chinese emperor wanted. When the Mongols arrived at the battlefield that the Chinese had prepared, they were forced to set up some of their siege equipment to use against the fortifications. While these weapons were being readied, the Chinese charged the Mongol position.

The journey had been long and tiring, but the Mongols had not been in battle for a long time. They were eager to engage their old enemies. For eons, the Chinese had exerted their superiority over the nomads, and in the days since the rule of Jenghiz Khan, the Mongols had enjoyed numerous opportunities to undo the Chinese in battle. No longer could the Chinese repel the attacks of the barbarians from the north.

The arrows flew, and the Chinese were the first to fire artillery. The Mongols were used to improvisation during battle, so they wasted no time waiting. They began to charge in and attack, and then retreat in coordinated efforts. After a few rounds of charge and retreat, the catapults were assembled, and the barrage began. When the center of the Chinese force was weakened, the Mongols charged through with arrows flying and swords drawn.

Straight Arrow was thrown from his horse by a boulder that came flying into the ranks of the Khan's army. It completely crushed two men and their horses, and the force of impact knocked Straight Arrow off of his terrified mount. He-Who-Goes-First saw what happened, and he retrieved his son's horse before continuing the battle. Straight Arrow rode to the rear of the fighting to collect his senses. His ears were still ringing as he tried to recover.

The battle was furious, and the Chinese did well at the beginning. If not for their armor, He-Who-Goes-First and his mare would have both been mortally injured. As it was, they were the bringers of death to many of the emperor's soldiers that day. At one point, He-Who-Goes-First lost his sword when he was hit hard in the arm. He pulled his battleaxe and continued to chop through his enemies.

The wise men and monks who spent their evenings in discussion with He-Who-Goes-First watched in horror and amazement as the

Mongols turned the tables on the Chinese and defeated them on their own battlefield. As He-Who-Goes-First recovered his sword and rode back to check on his son, the learned men were taken aback by the blood that stained him and his horse. Never before had these men witnessed such a battle. They stared in amazement, and one of the Indians staggered a few steps from his friends and began to vomit.

The monks were having second thoughts about their association with these ruthless warriors. The Indians knew that it was too late to undo their promise to meet the Khan. Slowly, as the dust settled and the blood soaked into the battlefield, they realized that they were still safe.

Straight Arrow would survive, though he had taken quite a jolt. His head ached, and his ears were still ringing, but he would recover. He-Who-Goes-First was bruised, but he and his mare were relatively unscathed after they washed off the blood of the Chinese. Without wasting any more time, they collected their own weapons and supplies and those that they had captured. The Chinese spoils were loaded onto Chinese horses, and the Khan's army continued their journey home. They had literally marched over and through the formidable force that the emperor had sent to greet them. Jenghiz would not be pleased by the emperor's audacity.

The Mongols were not far from home now, and when word reached Jenghiz Khan about the attack on his army, he assembled a force and led it south to meet his other, returning army. The messenger brought news that both forces would meet and surround the Chinese emperor. It would be a glorious victory and an appropriate ending to the long campaign that He-Who-Goes-First and his brothers had been on.

The days passed quickly as the two armies of the Khan closed on the emperor's palace. As planned, the Mongols surrounded the palace and destroyed it completely. The siege and battle were somewhat anticlimactic, since the emperor had fled earlier, after his army had been defeated on the battlefield. He was smart enough to know that Jenghiz Khan would lead an army and personally oversee the destruction of everyone and everything at the Imperial Palace.

Despite the disappointment, the Khan's attention soon turned to the men of knowledge that accompanied his brave soldiers on their return from the long campaign. Jenghiz Khan had an impressive communications system for the era he lived in. He had been notified weeks ago about the learned men who were coming to see him.

In full view of the decimated palace, the two Mongol armies set up camp. The next day, the new army would continue on, while the returning army would finish the journey to their homeland. That evening, Jenghiz resisted the urge to monopolize his foreign guests, and instead, the Khan decided to spend the evening around the fire with these men and He-Who-Goes-First and Straight Arrow. The group was so large on this night, that they built a giant bonfire and continued burning remnants of the Chinese palace long into the night.

He-Who-Goes-First waited for the Khan to start the discussion, as it only felt right for the leader to take charge. Jenghiz began by ordering kumiss to be brought for all who wanted it. He knew how to get things started. Then he asked the Indians and Tibetans to start a discussion. The men seemed unsure at first, since the reputation of the Khan was rather intimidating. Jenghiz was aware that his position was unnerving to the others, so he suggested that he was with his brothers on this night.

"We are camped under the sky enjoying a fire that we have made from the belongings of the cowardly emperor!" he shouted. "Let us enjoy this night! Please, continue with your discussion as you have done for so many nights before this one."

Slowly, the men began talking of matters of the spirit. The Khan noticed that the wise men and the monks had accepted He-Who-Goes-First and Straight Arrow into their group, and they even depended on He-Who-Goes-First to propel the discussion. The warrior had a way of asking thought-provoking questions and imparting his uncorrupted insight into the mix. With no formal education, He-Who-Goes-First had wisdom not unlike the Khan's. Soon Jenghiz and He-Who-Goes-First were leading the educated foreigners into the spiritual realm of the people from the Mongolian Steppe.

As the night continued, one of the Indian mystics asked He-Who-Goes-First if he had a story. The other soldiers murmured in agreement. The day had been long and now that the kumiss had loosened things up, they craved a humorous story before they retired.

He-Who-Goes-First let out a long sigh, and then he began to speak. From beyond the immediate glow of the firelight, Soonok sat in the shadows and listened to the laughter. He did not dare to speak against He-Who-Goes-First while he was enjoying the attention of the great Khan. The whole scene made Soonok very envious. Though he had recovered from the beating he had taken after provoking He-Who-Goes-First, he had never recovered from his anger.

As the group around the fire started to break up and head for their blankets, the Khan told He-Who-Goes-First and Straight Arrow that they would accompany him and the foreigners back to his palace. He said there was still much for them to discuss.

Chapter 20: Honored Guests

He-Who-Goes-First and the others arrived with Jenghiz Khan at the Khan's palace. Since they were all honored guests, no comfort was too large or too small. Straight Arrow had never seen such a place as this before. He was as overwhelmed as his father had been during his first visit years before.

Each guest was given a room with everything he could have desired. There were women, attendants and much food and drink. He-Who-Goes-First told his son to enjoy himself, and then he retired to his own room. Inside, he found that there was a warm bath waiting for him. He lay in the warm water, as beautiful women washed him and fed him. It was a treat like no other, for a man who had been on a military campaign for so long.

He indulged himself as much as he was able, before at last falling asleep on the comfortable bed that had been prepared for him. He awoke the next morning and found new clothes and more food waiting for him. An attendant appeared to see if he needed anything, and then informed He-Who-Goes-First that the Khan was expecting him at a reception in the great hall at midday.

At the appointed time, he was led into the hall and seated with the Khan, the three mystics, the two monks and his son. Straight Arrow beamed when he saw his father. He-Who-Goes-First could tell that he had been enjoying himself. The life of a soldier was a hard one. Not many had the opportunity to enjoy such opulence.

The Khan was ready to get down to business. He had attendants bringing food and drink, and a scribe to chronicle the important points of the discussion that they were about to have. Among the finery in the palace, the Khan had many beautiful plants and exotic birds and animals. A small monkey sat nearby, and the Khan would periodically toss it a nut or a piece of fruit. Several hounds had free run of the room, and one of them seemed to have taken a liking to He-Who-Goes-First. The dog sat near the warrior as He-Who-Goes-First patted its neck and stroked its fur.

There was wine, which He-Who-Goes-First found was even better than kumiss. All the luxuries that one could imagine, and some that they couldn't, were available. At the far end of the giant room, musicians played. At one point, Jenghiz found that he was having difficulty hearing his guests, so he ordered that they play quieter. He also had the attendants make adjustments to the amount of lighting in the room. Finally, when he was satisfied that all was right, he began to ask questions of the learned men.

The discussion began with the idea of the passage of time and how a ruler would be viewed by the people who would live in the future, long after his reign. They discussed some historical figures and tried to grasp how these individuals had appeared to their families, their enemies and their subordinates. Many such rulers were paranoid of treachery within their own families, and they often had good reason to be.

The Khan said that he valued both honesty and loyalty. Those who were disloyal were dealt with by the harshest means available. Loyalty, on the other hand, was rewarded and was the basis for success. Jenghiz asked He-Who-Goes-First if he had any objections to the Mongol ruler's tactics or decisions. This was a dangerous question, and the answer needed to reflect honesty, loyalty and preferably agreement with the Khan.

He-Who-Goes-First answered that he had, from time to time, thought about the duties of a soldier and the killing and subjugation of other peoples. He said that the wisdom of the Khan was that he offered a choice to those whom he invaded. It was clear that to obey the Khan was a policy that left one to live much as he always had. There were none of the usual religious restrictions that were characteristic of a takeover. Often, under the rule of the Khan, there was actually an increased sense of security. For those who rebelled or opposed the Khan, there was only death and destruction. He-Who-Goes-First argued that such a clear policy actually prevented many battles due to the knowledge of the futility of fighting against the armies of Jenghiz Khan.

The Khan seemed to be satisfied with this answer, and he questioned the foreign guests about their impressions of his soldiers and their prowess in battle. One of the Indians remarked that he had never seen such a formidable army ever before. The monks were pacifists, and they said that their spiritual beliefs did not condone war, yet they were impressed that a soldier such as He-Who-Goes-First had an intellectual and spiritual dimension that surpassed that of many men who were advocates of peace.

The Khan turned his attention to Straight Arrow.

"You," he said, "who has mastered the art of the bows. What have you to say about war and peace?"

Straight Arrow adopted his father's contemplative posture, and then he commented that there was neither good nor bad in what they did. It was as it had always been. The strong dominate the weak whether they are man or beast.

"Excellent!" remarked the Khan. "It is like this, my friends. Before my time as ruler, there was much fighting. Brother fought with brother, and neighbor stole from neighbor. My own wife was carried away many years ago, and I was forced to make war to get her back. It is always sweeter to take that which belongs to another. His women look more beautiful, and his gold shines more brightly. Once you have taken his land from him, you see that it is no better and no worse than that which you already possessed. The mere act of taking it away and possessing it for yourself is something that is basic and primitive." He continued. "My people, those who live in felt tents have always had warrior tendencies. We had no permanent dwellings, and the quest for a place to put your tent or build your fire or graze your animals has always existed. Those who had permanent homes walled us out. They looked down on us because we did not have gold and palaces.

Then we united under my command, and we took the things that we had never had before. We became powerful, because we are strong and we are now banded together as brothers, like the wolf who is our ancestor. The wolf does not mourn for the hare he has slain. He follows his spirit just as the people of the steppe do. We are strong, and now we have found our place at the top of the order."

The others were silent, not knowing what to say. It was He-Who-Goes-First who first spoke.

"It is as the Khan has spoken. Life has always been hard, and men have always killed and died. We are no better or no worse than they are. We are just more powerful. Life is better for our people since we no longer fight with each other. We have directed our efforts, and we have learned many things in the process."

The men nodded, and Jenghiz clapped his hands to signal the attendants to refill the cups and bring more food. He tossed another morsel to the monkey, and then he looked at his guests and said, "I would like to hear from all of you, what you think happens to a man after he releases his spirit to the wind. Where does he go after death?"

The conversation continued until they all needed a break because of too much wine and full bladders. They retired to their respective rooms for more sleep and indulgences. This routine continued for three days, until which time He-Who-Goes-First asked the Khan if he and his son could return home to their families. The Khan replied that they were free to return home whenever they wished, and He-Who-Goes-First requested that they part the following morning.

The next morning, washed, fed and wearing new clothes, father and son said their goodbyes to the Khan and his foreign guests. Outside, they found their horses, camels and assorted gifts from Jenghiz Khan to his honored brothers. The two mounted up, and He-Who-Goes-First was glad to be back on his favorite gray mare. She looked like she had been well cared for, but she seemed glad to be back with her favorite warrior.

The journey home took a couple of days, and it was uneventful. The two travelers were back in familiar territory, and they had been well provisioned for the journey. When they finally reached the settlement of their wives, they wished each other well and went to reacquaint themselves with their families.

Chapter 21: Homebodies

Gerka was waiting when He-Who-Goes-First arrived. Straight Arrow's son had seen the two warriors returning, and he had alerted their families. The other soldiers had been back for many days already, and at first Gerka had been afraid that her husband had died in battle in some far-off land. She was informed by the others that both He-Who-Goes-First and Straight Arrow had been invited to the Khan's palace. She knew that this was a great honor that he could not refuse, yet she was aware of the slight resentment that she harbored against him for not returning immediately.

She knew that her feelings were illogical, but it is not always easy to control one's feelings. When she finally laid eyes on her husband's round face, she felt as if she might faint. He-Who-Goes-First was so happy to see her that he slipped his arm around her waist and pulled her into the ger. He was not going to wait.

That night as he held his wife, she lay with her head on his chest. She had not offered any resistance to him. She seemed happy to have him back. He-Who-Goes-First was filled with joy to be back with his wife. For so long he had worried about what her reaction to him would be. She had said very little, but he knew that she was not one to show a lot of emotion. She had not tried to stop his advances or push him away. She willingly accepted him back into her life. She slept on his chest now, breathing in the scent of his body. All was well between them.

He stroked her hair as she slept. She was still the most beautiful woman he had ever seen. On so many nights, he had wished he could be doing just what he was doing now. He was happy again and more in love with her than he had ever been before.

He-Who-Goes-First was overwhelmed by his daughter's growth. She had, by this point, fully mastered the art of conversation. He was delighted to sit with her and her faithful dog, Edge, and talk about all the things that she wondered about. The child was curious and smart. She had learned many things from her mother during He-Who-Goes-First's absence. She was also becoming very helpful as a caretaker of their animals.

The little girl was intrigued by her father's and brother's new camels. She pleaded with He-Who-Goes-First to take her for rides on the large beast. One afternoon the girl came running into her mother's ger in a fit of hysterical laughter. She motioned for Gerka to follow her, and when they went outside, He-Who-Goes-First was riding the camel facing backwards! He was pretending to be befuddled by his predicament, and even his usually stoic wife burst into laughter when she saw him. He continued to ride around the village this way, until all the children were laughing and following him. When he finally righted himself, he made the camel kneel, and he reached down and pulled his wife and daughter onto its back.

The camel rose to its feet, and He-Who-Goes-First walked it slowly around. His daughter wanted to go faster, and soon they were hanging on tightly as the camel ran around the outside of the settlement. It was a wonderful afternoon that they all enjoyed very much.

The families of He-Who-Goes-First and Straight Arrow spent much of their time together. It was easier to maintain their livestock and take care of the many chores when they worked together. The wives of the two men had come to rely on each other heavily when their husbands were off to war. Straight Arrow's son was growing stronger, and he was very valuable to the families for his skills in caring for the horses. He was already a good horseman, and he liked to race the other boys of the village.

Life was good, and He-Who-Goes-First was grateful for the time with his family. He was enjoying this time, but inside he was feeling another internal struggle. Perhaps he should see if he could resign from the Khan's army and try to spend more time with his family. He was not sure if his resignation would be accepted or not. With military campaigns throughout the empire, he had a duty to do his part. Still, he had served in the Khan's military for a long time now, and he had fought in many battles. How many was enough?

He also wondered if this nomadic herding and hunting life would become tedious after a while. He had seen much of the world since he had first begun riding with the Khan's army. The experience had made him aware of many new and fascinating things. There was much to think about. He talked to Straight Arrow, who understood his father's feelings. He reminded He-Who-Goes-First that the soldiers enjoyed a status and wealth that was better than those who were not warriors. His father was not yet old, but he was reaching an age where he could probably resign his commission in a few more years.

Gerka wanted him to stay with her and their child, yet she secretly worried that if he was always present, she might become frustrated with him. She had little time over the last few years to do anything but miss her husband, yet the last occasion when he was home had not been very pleasant.

From all of his own soul-searching, He-Who-Goes-First finally concluded that perhaps it was slightly premature for him to give up being a soldier right now. Maybe if he went on one more campaign, he would have just cause to ask the Khan to allow him to leave his position. There was, of course, the chance that he would not return from another campaign. This was the risk that any soldier took, and it did not weigh too heavily on the decision. What was to happen would happen.

The time spent at home was not all domestic bliss. The settlement was mobile, and the whole village moved seasonally to find good grazing for their animals. There was also work to be done, such as milking and butchering. Now that they were home, He-Who-Goes-First and his son took over the duties of killing the animals that they needed for food. The work of cutting the meat, cooking and curing the hides was still done by the women, who also made the clothes.

This arrangement provided for significant free time for the soldiers who found themselves home with a family and a settlement that was fully capable of doing without them. The self-sufficiency of the women was a tribute to both their ingenuity and the status that women held in Mongol society. Women in this culture were afforded the right to divorce and also to decide for themselves if they wanted to remarry after becoming a widow. They were valued for their intellect as well. Even Jenghiz Khan listened to his wife Borte when she offered him advice. There was no stigma about this.

Perhaps, thought He-Who-Goes-First, his place really was with the army. This family life was a good one, but he was a warrior. He was perhaps the greatest of the Khan's swordsmen. It was his duty to use his talent to the benefit of the Khan and the empire. To do less would dishonor himself and his family. Once again, he had settled the struggle within his mind. He would enjoy this domestic life as long as he could, and when the day arrived to leave with his brothers, he would go.

As the weather grew colder, snow began to fall. Winter was always a challenge for the people, but He-Who-Goes-First found in it the opportunity to have some fun. He selected one of his strongest horses—one that he had used for pulling and dragging in the past. He fitted it with a harness made of skin, and he fastened it with rope to a hide that was stretched over a frame. He climbed onto the back of the horse, and as he rode it through the fresh snow, it pulled the makeshift sled behind it.

He-Who-Goes-First told his daughter and the son of his son that they could climb into the sled and he would take them for a ride. The children needed no further encouragement. They climbed into the sled and were soon speeding across the landscape laughing loudly. This went on for a while, and soon the other children of the village eagerly waited for their turns. Soon after that, the young boys were devising their own versions of this game. Sleds were being pulled by a variety of animals including sheep and goats.

Gerka watched along with Straight Arrow's wife, as their husbands played with the children. Obviously these two men had not outgrown their fondness for silly games. In the end, the two warriors even persuaded their wives to go for a ride. Finally, He-Who-Goes-First unhitched the large horse that had provided the muscle behind all the fun that they had. He rubbed it down and released it with the others. It had been another enjoyable day, due to a great warrior who also had a great capacity for having fun.

He-Who-Goes-First enjoyed the winter months. Despite the cold outside, there was a warmth from his family that he often missed while he was working to expand the empire. As the days grew longer and warmer, he spent his time teaching his daughter how to ride horses. He would also take Gerka for rides. Sometimes the two would leave their daughter with Straight Arrow and his wife, and they would ride off together. They enjoyed these rides, and they both knew that it was only a matter of time before He-Who-Goes-First would need to leave again.

Straight Arrow and his wife also liked to ride together, and occasionally they could talk their son into staying behind with He-Who-Goes-First and his family. The boy would beg his grandfather to teach him how to use a sword. He-Who-Goes-First had made two wooden practice swords, and they were often engaged in mock battle. When He-Who-Goes-First grew tired of this, he would pretend to be mortally wounded by the wooden sword. Then he would fall down and remain still while his grandson and daughter tried to revive him.

While he enjoyed his time with the children, it was Gerka who he was most in need of. Since he had returned, they had reconciled their relationship, and it was as strong as it had ever been. For all of his physical strength, He-Who-Goes-First had no difficulty in expressing his love for his wife. She was more reserved. She had become less able to express her feelings over the years. The more her husband was off to war, the more she protected herself against emotional injury.

Both knew that the long spans of time that He-Who-Goes-First was away could mean that death would separate them forever…at least until reincarnation could bring them back together again. He-

Who-Goes-First dealt with this knowledge by savoring every moment that he had with his wife. Gerka dealt with it by shielding her emotions from what had not yet happened.

Her failure to express her feelings had, at times, wounded He-Who-Goes-First deeply. He had learned, however, that this was how she reacted to his dangerous occupation. It was why he had considered resigning from the army early. He was not sure if this would remedy the situation or if the behavior had been permanently established. He was aware, however, that even though Gerka was not always able to show her true feelings, she did love him. This realization, along with his intense love for her, was enough for him to keep trying.

The winter had been exceptionally pleasant as far as their relationship was concerned. Only now as spring intruded did he notice his wife's mood grow more distant. They both dreaded the day that he would leave, yet something inside of the warrior also desired the excitement of battle.

The night before he departed, Gerka tossed and turned next to her husband, who lay still, but awake. A single tear ran out of his eye and down his face. The sadness they both felt was overwhelming, but the life of a Mongol was hard, and this was the sacrifice that must be made.

In the morning, He-Who-Goes-First and Straight Arrow readied their horses and supplies. This time, Straight Arrow's son would travel along with them and watch over the horses of his father and grandfather. The boy was excited about this step toward manhood. He would soon be tested, not only physically, but also emotionally when he witnessed the carnage of his first battle.

The women watched as their men rode off. Sadly they stared as the horses continued on, away from the village. In the doorway of her ger, Gerka stood holding the hand of her daughter as they watched He-Who-Goes-First ride away. They both stood motionless. The little girl was quiet and held her mother's hand for support. Gerka stood watching the horses and the men leaving as a single tear rolled down her cheek. She had a bad feeling this time. Somehow she knew that her husband would not be coming back.

Chapter 22:
The Life of a Warrior

The men tried to keep their minds off of the families that they had left behind. The first day was full of separation and intrigue about what lay ahead. He-Who-Goes-First was always surprised by the variety of feelings that he had in these situations. The ache in his heart was real. It was a separation pain that he felt from being away from Gerka. It was the realization that if he did see her again, he would have to wait months or even years.

As he thought about the challenges of battle that lay before him, he could feel the power coursing within his body. He had maintained his strength and agility through his daily training routines. He had also had sufficient time to heal all of his injuries. The realization dawned on him that while he was strong in mind and body, his emotions were now suffering from the injury of separation.

The gray mare was walking behind the stallion he was riding. He-Who-Goes-First liked to give his horses a break from carrying his weight. Indeed, that was why each soldier had several mounts with him. Straight Arrow rode nearby, and his son rode behind him. The boy had offered no complaints even when the trail became difficult. He was filled with wonder about what lay ahead. On this first day, he had already traveled farther from his birthplace than he ever had before.

The army traveled for many days until at last they were informed by their scouts that there was a hostile force up ahead. The news brought a mixture of feelings to He-Who-Goes-First. He had not been in battle for many months. There was always a slight nervous feeling before one rode headlong into a life or death struggle. On the other hand, he could feel the excitement pulsing through his veins with every beat of his heart.

They were ready, and when the moment arrived, the warriors rode into the enemy with great precision. The army was comprised mostly of men who had been in battle before; but even the newest of the Mongol warriors were well trained and exceptionally brave. He-Who-Goes-First was on his gray mare when they charged out ahead of the others. Moments before he made it to the skirmish line, his horse stopped and reared up. That was when He-Who-Goes-First noticed the pikes propped up against the ground.

He quickly gave warning to his fellow soldiers before they impaled their horses on the vicious spears that were aimed at their approach. He-Who-Goes-First jumped from his mount, followed by many others. They chopped their way through the men who held the cumbersome pikes until the sharpened poles lay harmlessly on the ground. The Mongols remounted their horses and charged ahead. It was this ability to react to unforeseen danger and the brilliant means of communication and organization that could leave their adversaries' best laid plans useless.

From behind the lines, Straight Arrow's son watched his father gallop across the battlefield and launch his arrows with deadly accuracy. In the midst of all the fighting, he saw his grandfather, He-Who-Goes-First, stained with the blood of his opponents as he darted to and fro on his gray mare. The horse had been the first to recognize the danger of the pikes, a split second before He-Who-Goes-First noticed them. She was truly an amazing animal, and her instincts may have saved the lives of many horses and men that day.

The boy was wide-eyed as he was initiated into the blood and death of warfare. He was alarmed by the danger his father and grandfather were in, as well as the death that littered the ground beneath their horses' hooves. Even though he had heard the stories of battles, it was quite unnerving to witness one for the first time. As he watched the fighting continue, he noticed that there were now vultures circling in the sky. He felt slightly dizzy, but he knew that he would have to remain strong. He was a proud Mongol, and he would survive this day only to become stronger.

The battle continued for a long time before the enemy became disorganized, terrified and began a full retreat. Few escaped as the Mongols relentlessly pursued their victims. Those who did get away, swore that the numbers of their attackers were two or three times more than what they actually were.

When Straight Arrow finally walked out of the battle, his son saw that his father was uninjured, though he was now on foot. Straight Arrow told him that his horse had been killed. It was several more minutes before He-Who-Goes-First emerged from the battlefield, covered in blood. His gray mare galloped up to Straight Arrow and the boy. They had survived the first battle of the campaign, and it was another victory for the Khan.

That evening, the boy marveled as his father and grandfather laughed with the others around their fire. They seemed largely unaffected by the violence of the day. It was at that moment that the boy resigned himself to emulate these two men. He would do his duty to the best of his ability, until one day, he too would ride into battle for the Khan.

A few days later, Jenghiz Khan arrived on the scene. He was going to accompany the army as it laid siege to the city of a certain nearby ruler. This was the third time that He-Who-Goes-First had met the Khan in person. The warrior and the ruler greeted each other warmly. Straight Arrow's son was in awe of both the reputation of this great leader and the fact that he was his grandfather's friend.

As the two men spoke to each other, the boy noticed a hawk circling in the sky above. He didn't know why, but he was sure that the hawk's presence was part of this fantastic event. As the boy continued to watch the bird, it appeared as if it flew right into the sun. The boy squinted into the bright light, waiting to see the hawk emerge out of the glare, but it was gone. It was no longer visible anywhere in the sky. The Khan spent that evening near the fire with He-Who-Goes-First and Straight Arrow. There was much that they had to talk about.

The Khan stayed with the army, and he took command. He had a personal score to settle with a certain ruler, and he intended to watch this man's world crumble before him. He moved his force forward until they reached the walled fortifications. The Khan's messenger was not admitted into the city, and the chance to avoid a battle had now passed. The ruler knew that he would not survive the Khan's wrath even if he gave up and opened the gates. Given that his own fate was already determined, he was not concerned about the impact of his decision on the rest of the inhabitants.

Jenghiz had hoped for such a result. He was prepared to destroy or carry off every piece of this kingdom. He wanted to make the necessary preparations so that once the assault began, it would be massively destructive and the fall would be quick. He ordered that the army surround the palace and set up the artillery. The soldiers would camp there for the night. The resulting fear that the wait would instill was only to the Khan's advantage. He also intended to participate in some of the nocturnal preparations.

That night, the Khan invited He-Who-Goes-First to accompany him on a pre-battle mission. There were two groups of men involved, and each group had two men who were trained in the use of gunpowder. This was another technological advancement that the Khan had originally acquired from the Chinese. It seemed that there was always someone who could be persuaded to give secrets away, if he was tempted by riches.

He-Who-Goes-First wasn't sure exactly what caused it to work, but he had seen the result of gunpowder in the past. Now he watched as the two demolitions experts dug holes and placed the bamboo canisters under the wall. On the other side of the city, another group was involved in the same activity. Inside the walls, the inhabitants were readying themselves for the inevitable attack by the Mongols. After the explosives were placed, the Khan and He-Who-Goes-First returned to their camp to finish preparations and to try to get some sleep. The attack would take place just before sunrise.

When morning came, the Khan ordered the charges to be lit. The explosions were terrifying, and the walls were cracked by the concussions. The Khan ordered the catapults to be fired. They were filled with more charges, flaming bales and boulders. The assault continued with battering rams, until at last, the walls were shattered. The army moved on the city, and most of the population was killed within the first few minutes.

The looting began, and food, supplies, women and animals were removed in great quantities. The assault continued with the complete destruction of all that had been previously enclosed inside of the walls. When the ruler was found, he was bound and placed so that he was crushed under a huge slab of his own wall. The Khan was pleased. He later told his men that there was no greater pleasure than to destroy one's enemies and take all that was dear to them.

The men were intoxicated by the victory and by the presence of the Khan himself. It was a good day to be a warrior in the army of Jenghiz Khan. The revelry continued for the rest of the day and into the evening. By the next morning, all that remained of the city and palace was rubble and ash. The Khan had made good on his promise to destroy this enemy completely.

The following day, the Khan took leave of the main army and rode with a fully loaded caravan back toward his palace. He-Who-Goes-First said goodbye to the Khan, and he promised to visit the palace again when he returned from the campaign. He-Who-Goes-First and his brothers continued their quest, and the two groups separated.

Straight Arrow's son was adapting to his new situation well. He was excellent with the horses, and he continued to practice his skills with the new weapons his father had given him. No longer was he using the wooden sword. He now had the real thing. His grandfather continued to show him the finer points of how to use the new weapon. The boy was also learning how to shoot his bows from the very best, his own father.

Life developed into a routine of travel and conquer. Sometimes the Mongols were able to exert the Khan's influence without the use of force, and sometimes they were required to conquer their enemies by military action. There were multiple armies at work within the empire, with several different leaders. Most of these leaders were related to the Khan by blood. It became apparent to He-Who-Goes-First that not all of these factions got along too well. If something were to happen to the aging Khan, the unity of the people might be severed.

There was nothing for him to do about this, but it might be necessary to identify the strongest leader at some point in the future. If there was a civil war, it would only be wise to be on the winning side. Hopefully that would never happen. If the Mongols began fighting with each other as they had in the old days, much of what Jenghiz Khan had accomplished could be lost.

Among his own ranks, there was only one man that He-Who-Goes-First still hated. It was the man Soonok. He had not challenged He-Who-Goes-First again after his beating, yet he was never very far away. His presence was unnerving, but there was no clear resolution for this in the near future.

The next few weeks were marked by rainy weather. The travel was difficult, and the men, horses and their supplies were always soaked. Many of the men and animals became ill, and some of them even died along the way. The morale of the troops was beginning to decline, but then the weather cleared just in time. During the first few sunny days, the army took a break from traveling and aired everything out. The sunshine and wind was put to use drying all of the clothing, blankets and supplies. As the puddles dried up and the mud solidified, travel was resumed.

The soldiers soon regained their appreciation for competitive games. The pleasant, warm days allowed them to race their horses and have wrestling and shooting competitions. With no battles in their immediate future, the men relied on these diversions to avoid boredom.

As the journey continued, the army arrived at a small village that appeared to be very poor. There was a noticeable lack of grown men in this land, and the warriors were soon directed by the inhabitants to a mass grave near their village. They were told by the people of this village that a powerful warlord lived in a city nearby. Though they offered him no resistance, his soldiers routinely invaded, attacked and looted the village. They expected him to attack again soon, since he had not done so for nearly an entire lunar cycle.

It took little persuasion from the Khan's envoy to convince this little hamlet to swear their allegiance to Jenghiz Khan. As it was now subject to the rules of the Khan, it also fell under the protection of the empire. The soldiers camped at the village, and they shared their food with the inhabitants. The lack of men was an added bonus for an army that had been on campaign. The soldiers rebuilt many of the structures that had been demolished by the warlord. As luck would have it, he arrived to take advantage of the town while the army was still there.

The warlord had his own army, which, while it was more than a match for a town of women, children and old men, was not prepared to take on the army of Jenghiz Khan. They quickly found themselves outmatched, and they began to retreat like the cowards that they were. The Khan's soldiers had not been in battle for a long while, and they took the opportunity to pursue this enemy all the way to their stronghold.

The entirety of the warlord's men made their last stand at this place, and the eager Mongols surrounded them and put them all to death, except for one. The warlord was captured alive, and he was bound with ropes and returned to the village he had so often decimated. The people of the village were overwhelmed by their sudden liberation. They again swore their allegiance to Jenghiz Khan, and they thanked their new friends. As He-Who-Goes-First and the others rode away from the village, they could hear the cries of the once powerful warlord as the people dished out their revenge.

There were other small populations in the vicinity who also became instant allies of the force that had destroyed the warlord who had been tormenting them for so long. It was an unusual situation for the Mongols to be seen as liberators. The place where one ends up in history is often determined by the point-of-view of those who write it down. If these simple villagers had written the history of Jenghiz Khan's hordes, he would have undoubtedly been hailed as a great hero and liberator.

Such was not to be the case, however. The Khan generally wanted to subjugate all of the people that he came into contact with. Those who were not already under the control of a ruthless leader were not apt to look upon the conquering Mongols as heroes. From the viewpoint of most of these peoples, indeed they were not.

Chapter 23: Last Ride

The army had made it to the Sea of Japan. They camped near the shore, and the men enjoyed the view. They needed a rest, and this was a good place to stop. The only thing left to do now was to turn around and head west. They could dip down into China or maybe head up to the north toward Rus'. For the moment though, they were content to spend some time near the shore.

On the morning that they had planned to leave, a thick fog shrouded everything. The sun was blocked out, and from where they were camped, it was impossible to distinguish where the sky and the water met. Visibility was poor, and they made the decision to stay put. The humidity was high, and there was a slight chill in the air. Their clothes were damp, and the men were reminded of the rains that had plagued them a few weeks earlier.

The next day started out foggy, but the sun soon burned through. The Khan's army mounted up and started their journey back toward their homeland. This had been a relatively short and uneventful campaign so far. He-Who-Goes-First was secretly thinking about his personal situation and pondering the question of whether to seek a discharge from military service. He had been through so much war already. He was still a mighty warrior, but something inside of him wanted to leave the fighting behind and spend his latter years herding horses, goats and cattle on the steppe.

The fog had lifted, and he noticed an eagle flying high above. It reminded him of his childhood. He used to love to watch the eagles fly over the steppe while he tended to his father's horses. The sight was comforting to him. His boyhood world lay off in the distance, yet a little piece of that world was soaring just above him.

The eagle was up high, and it continued to make wide turns in the sky above the army. The sun felt warm, and it was a welcome relief from the dampness of the past couple of days. Now that they were heading back toward home, He-Who-Goes-First could feel the anticipation growing inside of him. He wanted to see Gerka and their daughter. Each time he left them, it became harder to endure the separation.

Straight Arrow was also eager to go home. Though his son traveled with him now, he missed his wife, and he knew that the boy missed his mother. His son walked that line between boyhood and manhood; and though this was a short campaign for the rest of the men, Straight Arrow knew that it had been like an eternity for his son. The boy had done well. He had cared for the horses and helped with the chores. He had also been brave while the battles waged. It was not an easy life. It would be good if his first trip could be a short one.

He-Who-Goes-First had another good reason to return home. His favorite gray mare had slowed down just a bit. It may have gone unnoticed by any other man, but He-Who-Goes-First and the mare were so in tune with each other that he could sense the slight hesitation and the minuscule decline in her stamina. He had a good idea why, but he was still not completely sure at this time.

He watched the sky and the eagle that had moved farther away up ahead toward home. It was as if it was leading them back to their homeland. The army continued on. He-Who-Goes-First rode his stallion with the gray mare in tow. He was lost in thought as he rode along. Life had been so difficult and so promising all at once. He was good at hiding his emotions while on campaign, but he had less control over them when he was with Gerka.

He had been born with a lot of emotion. He was deeply affected by all that he saw and heard. The only way that he had been able to survive within the harsh reality of the life of a Mongol warrior was by blocking out the screams and the pain as much as he could. While he was fighting battles with the army, he had learned to separate himself from the devastation that he helped to cause. On rare occasions, such as the time he witnessed the woman toss her child from the burning window and jump to her death, he was struck down by the tragedy that he witnessed. Most often, however, he was able to focus on the task at hand and filter out the unpleasantness that surrounded him. He was neither a cruel man, nor was he merciful on the battlefield. He was like his ancestor the wolf.

The self-discipline required to stabilize his emotions had taken immense energy and concentration. He had often wished that he could just let go and acknowledge his true feelings. That was something that he could never do on the battlefield. To show weakness would be to invite tragedy—and death. Only with Gerka and his daughter did he allow himself the luxury of showing the true depth of his emotions.

Those feelings of love and kindness were balanced by a dark side. This was the side that took over when Soonok had pushed him too far. He could have easily killed the man when he served up that beating the last time he was provoked. It was an emotion that was generally absent from his exploits on the battlefield. Only if he sought to end the life of one who had killed one of his brothers would he fight in anger. He charged into battle as one would react to a crisis. War was his job. As a soldier, he did his job in the same way that anyone who has a dangerous occupation would.

He had now reached a point in his life where he desired a less intense occupation. If only he could let his guard down a little and enjoy himself more. Sure, he had fun with his brothers around the evening campfire, telling stories and making jokes. This was, however, only a small refuge for him, into that place within his soul that wanted to have fun and share his emotions. It was hard to always be so tough!

He-Who-Goes-First had been daydreaming. His eyes were open, but the outside world had not been registering in his mind. His subconscious had taken over his senses -when suddenly he became aware of the movement of the horse beneath him. Upon regaining his state of alertness, he scanned the sky; looking for the outline of the eagle. It was gone. Sometime during his daydreaming, it had drifted away; out of sight.

He thought about his daughter. She had her mother's beauty, but she was very much like her father. She was an emotional child. He-Who-Goes-First was sometimes concerned about how deeply she was affected by things. He wondered if she could survive the danger and the sadness that life brought forth. He also knew that she was strong. Despite her tendency toward her father's emotions, she also possessed many of his characteristics for coping. She was a strong, happy girl. He should not worry so much. The best thing he could do for his daughter would be to return home safely.

After riding for a couple of days, the army turned and dropped to the south. There was another battle in their future. He-Who-Goes-First was now fighting the despair that he felt when they adjusted their course. He was no longer moving directly toward his family. They continued southwesterly, and soon they met the army that they had been sent to intercept. It was a huge force that was well outfitted. This would be no easy task, but the Mongols were now craving battle since they had been unchallenged for many weeks.

It was midday, and the opposition had wanted to wait until the next morning to engage. The Mongols were not in a waiting mood, however. Many of them felt as He-Who-Goes-First did. They had been moving toward their homeland and had suddenly been diverted. It seemed that only this army now stood between them and their families.

The fighting started, and He-Who-Goes-First was back on his gray mare. He had not ridden her much lately, and she was anxious to run. The initial assault began with the usual barrage of arrows. Then there was the call to charge. He-Who-Goes-First lead his ten into battle. He was first to ride into the fighting, as usual. The battle began with much difficulty. The Mongols were outnumbered, but the enemy troops were not as battle-hardened as the men of the Khan's army.

As the fighting erupted into a close quarter battle, the Mongols began to take the advantage. One of the men of his ten was struck down and lay bleeding on the ground. He-Who-Goes-First looked over just in time to see his brother crushed beneath the hooves of a horse. He could feel the rage building inside as he charged his mare into the fray and started cutting men down. During the fighting, one of the enemy soldiers swung his sword at He-Who-Goes-First, who ducked as the edge came at his head. The sword connected with the top of his helmet, knocking it off. He-Who-Goes-First found himself amidst the fighting with his head exposed.

There was no time to worry about his loss of equipment. He continued fighting and noticed that blood was running into his eyes. He was used to being covered in blood, but this time it was his own. Now more than ever, He-Who-Goes-First relied on that ability he had that allowed him to navigate in battle on instinct. Between his own instincts and those of his horse, he was able to continue killing the enemy until the battle had turned decisively in favor of the Khan's army.

That was when he heard the shout of his second in command of the ten. The man shouted for He-Who-Goes-First to go get help for his wound. Since the fighting was nearly over, He-Who-Goes-First rode his gray mare to the rear of the battle, where he sought the aid of a medic. Straight Arrow noticed his father leaving the battlefield, and he raced up on his horse in time to see the flap of skin that had lifted up and showed the exposed bone of He-Who-Goes-First's skull underneath.

Perhaps it was due to the intense bleeding, but the wound appeared clean, and the skin was pressed back into place, and his head was wrapped. Straight Arrow described the wound to his father and asked him if it hurt much. He-Who-Goes-First said he had not felt it, and only the blood dripping into his eyes had let him know that he had been injured. The fighting was all but over now, and the Mongols were either chasing the retreating survivors or helping the wounded off of the battlefield. It was then that He-Who-Goes-First saw his grandson riding toward him. The boy had found his grandfather's helmet, and he held it up in the air as he rode to where his father and grandfather were sitting. The boy handed the helmet to He-Who-

Goes-First, who nodded approvingly.

After he had time to lose the rush of adrenaline that usually accompanied his participation in battle, He-Who-Goes-First felt weak and dizzy. He needed a chance to rest, and he felt better after he had some food and water. He had lost a considerable amount of blood while exerting himself after his injury. He was in tremendous physical condition, however, and he soon felt much better.

That evening, despite his close call, He-Who-Goes-First entertained his brothers with stories and jokes around the campfire. It had not yet completely sunk in just how close to death he might have come. The laughter around the fire was his way of dealing with the adversity of life, and the inevitability of death.

Later, as he lay awake wrapped in his blanket, He-Who-Goes-First thought of Gerka and how badly he wanted to return to her. He could have lost his life earlier that day, and the thought of never seeing his wife again was not a good one.

The next morning, the bandage around his head was changed. The bleeding had stopped, and the medic was careful not to pull the flap of skin loose. It was not an easy injury to heal. There was nothing to suture, but the medic indicated that the wound appeared to look as good as could be expected. In reality, it was only the skin that was damaged. It was just the fact that it was hard to keep the wound closed so that it could heal properly.

The good news was that the army had now turned to the north. They were once again heading in the direction of home. It was a welcome thought to return from a campaign so soon. He-Who-Goes-First remembered the camp that the army had made near the shore of the Sea of Japan. Had it not been for the sea blocking the way to the east, they may have still been headed in that direction! With a little bit of luck, he would be home in a few weeks.

Since the weather was good and there were no enemies to challenge them, the army was able to make good time. Without many other outlets to vent their energy, the men participated in competitions whenever they could. He-Who-Goes-First was unable to participate in his preferred sport of wrestling, due to the wound on his head. It was healing nicely, but there was no reason to jeopardize that unnecessarily. He was happy to watch the competition. He did participate in an archery contest, but it was Straight Arrow who prevailed in this competition.

There was horse racing, but He-Who-Goes-First was reluctant to run his gray mare due to her recent condition. She was still not noticeably different to anyone else, but He-Who-Goes-First knew that something was growing inside of her. He refused to participate in horse racing, despite the continued invitations of the other men. He-Who-Goes-First told them that his horse had proven herself to be the best many times, and it was good for the other horses to have a chance.

This excuse worked for a while, but as the competition grew over the next few days, the men were anxious to see if the mare could still outrun all of the other horses. This debate did not concern He-Who-Goes-First. He had nothing to prove to anyone. All he wanted to do at this point was to heal from his injury and return home to Gerka and his daughter.

He-Who-Goes-First preferred to spend his free time by practicing with his sword. He could be seen at the edge of camp spinning, twirling and swinging his preferred weapon. He drilled daily, and the spectacle was quite impressive to watch. Straight Arrow's son liked to watch his grandfather's movements as he practiced with the sword. The speed at which he moved was so fast, that the sword was no more than a blur as it flew dangerously close to the body of the warrior who trained with it.

In the evenings, He-Who-Goes-First still enjoyed his time telling jokes and stories. As the days went on, however, he found his thoughts more and more with Gerka. She was so close now that he could almost feel her. Realistically, there were still several more days of travel ahead, but he was already with her in spirit.

The anticipation only grew as the army continued journeying toward home. The men tried to keep their minds off of their homecoming as best as they could. The competitions continued, as this kind of activity provided the best outlet for their frustrations. As the level of competition had been sorted out in the past few days, the men began to apply more pressure on He-Who-Goes-First to race his gray mare. Other men offered to ride her in the competition, but He-Who-Goes-First would not hear of it.

Soon they attempted to goad him into racing by suggesting that he no longer possessed the fastest horse. While these comments were bothersome, He-Who-Goes-First was still not ready to give in. Finally, he told the men that he would participate in one race of his choosing. He-Who-Goes-First set the course for the event, and then he spent a long time with his mare beforehand. He was sure that she could win, though he was also sure that she was not up to her usual potential. Still, it was time to put an end to the rumors and comments of the other soldiers.

As the horses all lined up before the race, the excitement of both man and beast was very high. There were 100 men on horseback, ready to charge across the landscape to determine who had the fastest horse. All were at the ready, and the general gave the command to begin.

The wall of horses shot forward as they began to juggle for position. He-Who-Goes-First and his mare were uncharacteristically not at the front when the race began. He did not want to push his mare too hard, but rather, he would let her take charge of her own pace. As the gray mare hit her stride, she stretched out and began to pull ahead of the others as her hooves punished the ground. The intensity of her focus was as unmatched as her speed, and He-Who-Goes-First had only to hold on as they began to put more distance between themselves and the other racers.

The finish line was just ahead, and by now He-Who-Goes-First and his mare were far ahead of the others. There was nothing left to do but cross the line and then run the mare back slowly to give her a chance to warm down. The gray horse and her rider crossed the line as the group of onlookers erupted into a frenzy of cheers. That was when it happened.

With a sudden jolt, He-Who-Goes-First fell from his mare while she was at a full run. He was lying on the ground still conscious as he felt the earth around him shake, and he could hear the thunder of 400 hooves beating against the hard ground. He looked up and saw the stocky men on their stocky horses running toward him. He was unconcerned, because he knew these men were his friends. He knew that he belonged with them. Suddenly, everything went dark.

Chapter 24:
The Aftermath

He-Who-Goes-First was startled when he regained his senses. He was no longer in the open country. There were no horses and no soldiers. He only saw his father, his mother and his brother, who was killed when they were both young. The three motioned for him to follow as they floated effortlessly toward a bright light in the distance. He tried to follow, but they disappeared before he could reach them. He continued on into the light until he found his father waiting for him.

"Where is this?" he asked his father.

"You have passed into the other world," his father told him. "You are no longer of the flesh; you are now of the spirit."

His father waved him on and then slowly evaporated into the mist that enveloped everything. He-Who-Goes-First was aware of the mist, but he also noticed that it was not wet. It was much like the fog that he had experienced as a flesh and blood man, but he was unaffected by any sensation of dampness now as a spirit.

The eagle was waiting just up ahead. It was as big as he had remembered it. The bird nodded to him, and He-Who-Goes-First climbed onto its back for his journey into the afterlife.

"What will happen to Gerka and our daughter?" he asked the eagle.

"They will join you, but they are not yet ready to leave," replied the eagle.

Satisfied, He-Who-Goes-First was somehow aware that everything was going to be alright. He was no longer overwhelmed by the feelings that he would never see his wife and daughter again. He knew that he would. The eagle pumped its wings, and the two rose higher and higher.

"Who are you?" asked He-Who-Goes-First, wondering if he was talking to God.

"I am the gatekeeper, the messenger and your tour guide," replied the eagle. "I am what you have made me. To you, the eagle is your sense of wonder and your stability."

"I was surprised to find an eagle in charge here," said He-Who-Goes-First.

"I am neither in charge, nor am I an eagle," the eagle answered. "I am an eagle to you, as I am a horse or a grandfather or a tree to someone else. I am the form that you see in me. As far as who is in charge…that is a concept that is quite different in this world from the way you knew it before. You will soon meet your past and look into your future. It is all in one here. Soon you will begin to remember who and what you are."

He-Who-Goes-First was suddenly seeing images of all that he had been as well as what was yet to come. He was overcome by a sense of understanding. He had found his reality. All of the questions made sense now. The answers could not travel into the flesh and blood world. To be all-knowing would be unfulfilling—like taking a test after being given the answers. Life was a process of learning. He now realized that he was not an uneducated man. He was, in fact, a wise spirit.

The eagle continued to carry the former warrior to his next adventure. There was no pain here. There was no sense of loss. There was no hate, and there was no death. There was only the satisfaction of accomplishment for a life well lived. He-Who-Goes-First felt warm. He was at peace.

* * * *

Gerka sat near the fire with her daughter and the wife of her son, Straight Arrow. She was suddenly overwhelmed by a sense of dread.

The attack of anxiety came on quickly, and it was debilitating. She cried out as pain shot through her chest and head. Her daughter-in-law rushed to her side just as Gerka fainted. Sweat glistened on her forehead, and she murmured softly as the other woman attempted to revive her.

Gerka's daughter was terrified. She had felt the sadness in her mother for many months, but she had never seen her like this. The mournful cry that erupted from Gerka just before she passed out was like that of an animal that had just been trapped and was waiting for the deathblow.

The girl ran for water and returned in time to see her mother regain consciousness. The woman and the girl looked at Gerka, waiting for some sign that she would be all right. Gerka struggled to speak. Slowly, she managed to sit upright. She stared into the fire as a single tear ran down her cheek.

"He will not come back," she told them.

* * * *

The shouting that had erupted was instantly silenced. The men stood staring in shock at what they had just witnessed. He-Who-Goes-First lay on the ground, just across the finish line. His eyes were still open, but he could no longer see. A puddle of blood was soaking into the dry ground beneath him. The earth drank his lifeblood as his flesh began to cool.

The gray mare had turned around when she felt her rider fall off. She walked slowly back toward her fallen friend. Straight Arrow had pushed his way through the group of onlookers and found his father lying dead on the ground. An arrow stuck out of his back, and the point had penetrated through his chest in the front. Straight Arrow was in disbelief, but he couldn't help but think that it was a good shot. His father's heart had been skewered by the arrow. Death had been quick.

With tears running down his cheeks, Straight Arrow looked up from the tragedy and shouted one word at the huge crowd of men who were standing in dumb silence.

"WHO?"

The crowd shifted as the eyes and heads of the soldiers began to turn. They all looked at a single man who was still holding the bow that he had used to commit his crime. It was Soonok. He had achieved his vengeance against the son of the man who had killed his father. In doing so, he had sealed his own fate.

Straight Arrow reached down and pulled the sword from the scabbard of his father's lifeless body. With tears still streaming from his eyes, he made his way toward the man who had taken his father's life. The crowd parted as the other men quickly moved out of the way.

As Straight Arrow covered the distance between his father's body and the man who had murdered him, the world appeared very different. He heard no sound, and time seemed to move in slow-motion. He was aware that he was moving, but the sensation seemed surreal. He focused on the man who had repeatedly attacked his father. The coward had finally resorted to shooting He-Who-Goes-First in the back.

Soonok stood motionless, unsure of what he should do next. He could run, but there was no way that he could escape the entirety of Jenghiz Khan's army. He watched as the son of the son of the man who had killed his father approached him. At the last moment, Soonok decided to pull his own sword. He pulled the weapon, and as he raised it, Straight Arrow swung his father's sword with both hands, horizontally at the exposed neck of Soonok. The force of the blow was as astounding as the hatred and rage that propelled it. It had come from deep within a son who had lost his father and his best friend just moments before.

Soonok's head and sword hit the ground at approximately the same time. His body followed a second later. Straight Arrow looked up into the sky, and he screamed the agony that was in his heart. The eagle heard the scream as it soared through the sky above. Below, there was a large group of men and horses, and the keen eyes of the bird could see that there was also death.

The son of Straight Arrow was still in shock. In the same moment that he had watched his grandfather win a horse race, he also saw an arrow pierce his back. There was no armor. There had been no reason to wear it for a horse race. Shortly after his grandfather had stopped moving, the boy had watched his own father strike down the man who had murdered He-Who-Goes-First, with a single, tremendous blow from his grandfather's own sword.

* * * *

It was a warm day. Straight Arrow was with his family outside, enjoying the pleasant weather. His wife was nearby. Her stomach was growing round as she carried the child that would be coming soon. Their son was out in the field with the horses.

The gray mare that had belonged to He-Who-Goes-First grazed with the other horses. A foal stood near to her. It had the same markings as its mother, only it was darker in color. Already the foal was showing much promise as it would gallop across the steppe with its mother. Straight Arrow prized the gray mare almost as much as his father had. She was a splendid animal, and so was her offspring.

Gerka mended clothing near the family's fire. Her daughter sat with her dog, Edge. The girl was teaching him to do tricks, and she liked to boast to the other children that hers was the smartest dog in the whole world.

Straight Arrow had welcomed his mother into his own family; and though she was not an old woman, Gerka had chosen not to remarry after the unfortunate death of her husband. She remained melancholy and preferred not to show her emotions in the presence of others. She missed her husband though, and she knew that somehow he was with her even now. The people of the steppe maintained strong ties to nature, and they carried the belief that the spirit could live on and even be reborn into another person after death.

Straight Arrow was making new arrows. He carefully crafted each one and then placed it in a pile with the others. Around his neck, he wore a necklace made from an ancient tooth strung on a piece of sinew. His father had worn it for as long as Straight Arrow had known him. His grandfather before him had worn it too. The tooth was a remnant from an ancient predator, long since dead. In time, Straight Arrow's son would wear the necklace. It was a testament to the power of time. Could a man really own something that would remain long after his death? These were the questions that He-Who-Goes-First had pondered while he was still alive. Now that he had passed into the other world, the necklace belonged to his son.

Gerka watched her daughter with the dog. She was glad to have the loyal animal as part of her family. It had provided much comfort to the girl after her father's death. Gerka's attention turned to the son of Straight Arrow, who was playing with the foal of her late husband's favorite gray mare. The boy and foal ran together across the ground, when all at once, the small horse took off and galloped in a wide circle as the boy watched and laughed.

Gerka missed her husband, and she was not ready to give her heart to another man. She would never be ready. She was comfortable living with her son's family. They treated her well and valued her as one of their own.

Gerka looked up into the sunlit sky. She saw an eagle soaring high above. It was something that she had taken more notice of lately. Her husband had been intrigued by the flight of these birds. She had sometimes caught him watching the sky, oblivious to the rest of the world. As she saw the eagle circle, she felt a warmth come over her. It was as if He-Who-Goes-First had placed his hot hand on her spine, and the heat flowed through her entire body. She kept working on her mending, and as she continued to watch the eagle, she didn't seem to realize that she was smiling.

* * * *

He was daydreaming. Oblivious to the world, the stress of trying to find a job and the frustration and depression of being out of work had been interfering with his sleep. He was qualified. He had gone to college, but the job that was supposed to be waiting for him after graduation was more than elusive.

His eyes were open, but his mind had taken control of his senses. It had transported him into a dream world—somewhere between the realms of sleep and wakefulness. The image came on without warning and with no apparent reason. Somehow, he was seeing a vision that had belonged to someone else. He found himself on the ground, feeling it vibrate and hearing the thunder of hundreds of hooves. He caught a glimpse of the stocky men riding their stocky horses toward him. He was not afraid. He felt as though he was a part of this group and they were coming to him.

That was when he came back to reality. He sat in stunned silence; reflecting on what had just happened. The vision had been vivid, complete with feelings that had permeated his soul. What was it, and what did it mean? Was it simply a case of his imagination taking some liberties?

He pulled himself back into his own world. He had things to do. The significance of what had just happened would not become fully evident until sometime later. It would slowly develop and come together into something that would forever change his life. It was not a good thing or a bad thing; it just was. In time, this mystery would help him to understand many things about himself.